"Because I w̶̶̶̶̶̶̶̶̶̶̶̶̶̶̶̶̶̶̶̶, too."
He moved the bottle to his lips and took a long drink.

She was mesmerized as he swallowed long and deep, head thrown back. He placed the bottle on the desk before his gaze landed on her. Her stare danced from his sculpted cheekbones to his sensuous lips and settled on his intense eyes, eyes that looked back at her as if he wanted to devour her for a meal, a meal that certainly ended with dessert.

She turned her back to him and felt him press up behind her. Gently pushing her hair aside, he kissed her tenderly on the neck. With a sweet moan she rolled her neck to the side to give him better access.

He knew he should be getting home. He knew he shouldn't be doing this right now. But none of that was going to stop him. He caressed her shoulders and eased the zipper down her long back, hoping he wasn't moving too fast, knowing he couldn't stop.

Books by Candice Poarch

Kimani Romance

Sweet Southern Comfort
His Tempest
Then Comes Love
Loving Spoonful

Kimani Arabesque

Family Bonds
Loving Delilah
Courage Under Fire
Lighthouse Magic
Bargain of the Heart
The Last Dance
'Tis the Season
Shattered Illusions
Tender Escape
Intimate Secrets
A Mother's Touch
The Essence of Love
With This Kiss
Moonlight and Mistletoe
White Lightning

CANDICE POARCH

fell in love with writing stories centered around romance and families many years ago. She feels the quest for love is universal. She portrays a sense of community and mutual support in her novels.

Candice grew up in Stony Creek, Virginia, south of Richmond, and now resides in northern Virginia. This year Candice and her husband will celebrate their thirty-second wedding anniversary. She is a mother of three and was a computer systems manager before she made writing her full-time career. She is a graduate of Virginia State University and holds a bachelor of science in physics.

Candice loves to hear from readers. Please visit her Web page at www.CandicePoarch.com or write to her at P.O. Box 291, Springfield, Virginia 22150.

LOVING
Spoonful

Candice Poarch

KIMANI™
ROMANCE

To my mother, Rev. Ethel Poarch, who has been
a phenomenal, loving role model to my sister and me,
as well as an inspiring community leader
for so many others.

KIMANI PRESS™

ISBN-13: 978-0-373-86114-9
ISBN-10:   0-373-86114-1

Recycling programs
for this product may
not exist in your area.

LOVING SPOONFUL

www.kimanipress.com

Printed in U.S.A.

Dear Reader,

Thank you for reading *Loving Spoonful,* the third novel in the SURPRISE, YOU'RE EXPECTING! Mother's Day series. I was overjoyed to participate in the series this year. Marriage and motherhood takes as much dedication and fortitude, not to mention love, heartbreak and joy, as any nine-to-five job.

Jack and Kimberly live in a fast-paced world in which it's so easy for the romance in a marriage to get lost among all the rest of life's concerns. As a couple becomes more comfortable together, change is expected, but to keep love alive, some of the joy and romance that brought them together in the first place needs to be as much a part of life as careers and other necessities.

I hope you enjoy your voyage with Jack and Kimberly.

And to all mothers everywhere, have a very happy Mother's Day.

With warm regards,

Candice Poarch

Prologue

It was Jack Canter's birthday, but it felt unlike any birthday he'd had in the past. There was no cake with festive candles, or the favorite meal his mother always prepared for all of them on that one day. No gifts, laughter or teasing. Instead, his mother's lips were pinched with worry. Her distress wrapped around him like a vise.

Something was definitely wrong. His stepfather had packed his bags and left a week ago, but Jack considered that a stroke of luck, not a loss. The man wasn't half the man Jack's father had been. Jack had known that from the moment he met the man.

"Mom, don't worry about gifts," Jack tried to reassure her. "I'm sixteen, almost a man."

"In your dreams," his brother Devin said with a trace of humor. Devin was a couple of years younger than he. Their mother had sent all the other kids to bed.

"What's wrong, Mama?" Jack asked, because she was having a hard time revealing her worries. He didn't understand her fixation on a man, but maybe she really missed his stepfather.

"All the money's gone. And if this real estate career doesn't work out, we're going to lose the house."

"Lose the…" Jack grabbed a breath. "Daddy left plenty of money. The house was paid off." In addition to the insurance policies that amounted to three hundred thousand, there were the college funds for each of them, and Jack knew there had been money in the bank. A couple of years ago, his mother had gone over their finances with Jack after his father died. Though he'd been barely in his teens, Jack had begun to work with his father, and his dad had gone over the finances with him very closely—treated him like a man.

"Your stepfather borrowed against the house."

"Everything's gone?" Devin asked.

Tears slipped from his mother's eyes. "Everything," she whispered, her sadness crushing down on them.

"How could that…?" Devin started, but Jack stopped him with a firm hand on his arm.

Now he understood why his mother had been taking those real estate classes. His stepfather hadn't worked at a single job for more than a month or so, after he married their mother a year ago. Something was always wrong. A boss always picking on him, or the work was too hard or damaging to his health, or he got laid off for some lame reason—according to him. But how did a man run through hundreds of thousands in a year?

"We'll make it, Mom," Jack assured her. "I'll get a job."

"Yeah, me, too," Devin murmured.

"But you're too young."

"We can deliver papers," Jack said with a smile he didn't feel. "I have my license and can get an after-school job, too."

"But all the money we saved up for your college is gone, too," his mother said.

The bottom fell out of Jack's stomach. He swallowed hard to keep the nausea back. While he'd worked side by side with his father, his dad told Jack how proud he was to save enough money for all his children's educations, and that he had a business that let him provide well for his family. And now it was all gone? His father had worked days and nights. He'd put in the hours of a person working two jobs. Jack couldn't believe his stepfather had run through all that—and so quickly.

After all that work, they had nothing but a mortgage to show for all his father's efforts. How hard did a man have to work—how much did a man have to save to ensure his family's future?

His mother sent them to bed after the talk, but for a week after, Jack couldn't sleep and could barely eat. Most of the time his stomach cramped with worry.

He saw how quickly something substantial could

become nothing. This sick, insecure feeling was eating out his insides. No matter what, he was determined nothing was going to make him feel like this again. His family would never want for anything, he promised.

Jack had found a job, but he'd also given up all his after-school activities. There would be no more hanging out with his friends, and he had to keep his grades up to make sure he got scholarships for college.

Chapter 1

It was Thursday, and Kimberly Canter was rushing to finish her dinner preparations. Her husband, Jack, had called earlier promising he'd join them—for a change—and she'd fixed his favorite beer-battered chicken. Although he could order it any time in one of their brewpubs, he'd always liked hers better. Kimberly heard the garage door rumble. He was home.

Jack had been disgruntled lately because Kimberly's part-time, morning weather forecaster job at a major Washington, D.C., television station had increased to full-time. During the week, she was at the station by three-thirty each morning, and since Jack worked most evenings and weekends, they rarely saw each other anymore. Rarely did he make it home until late, and both she and the children missed him terribly.

She missed Jack most of all. She missed going to bed with her husband sleeping beside her, instead of waking for work to find him fast asleep on the other side of the bed. Maybe tonight they'd close the door to their bedroom suite and retire early. She'd already put the CD in place and could envision the soft, sweet music piping throughout the room.

Jack breezed into the kitchen from the garage, his powerful, well-toned body moving with easy grace. He wore beige slacks and a black golf shirt with "Jack's Place" emblazoned in gold on the left breast. And he carried himself with a commanding air of self-confidence.

Kimberly's heart jolted and her pulse pounded as she stared with longing at him. Even at thirty-eight, Jack radiated seductive vitality. He hadn't lost any of his punch in the nearly seventeen years they'd been married. But they'd been without sex much too long now, and her body longed for intimacy.

A daily exercise regime kept his wide shoulders and six-one frame perfectly fit. Kimberly's gaze ran lovingly over him. His hair was cut short, and the shirt complemented his walnut complexion. Lord, he was still one great-looking man, and she was as in love with him today as she'd been when they started dating during her freshman year in college.

"Hi, honey," Kimberly said, with her hair pulled back in a ponytail and feeling dowdy by comparison. She'd planned to shower and dress in something a little sexy before he arrived. No such luck. What woman who worked full-time and had a couple of teenagers could ever get everything done on schedule? As soon as they got home she'd sent them upstairs to start on their homework.

"Hey. Something smells good. I can barely wait for dinner," Jack said before he passed her, barely glancing her way.

Suddenly deflated, Kimberly regarded his retreating back as he strolled out of sight. A kiss would have been nice, but Kimberly let that small lack of affection—something that had stopped lately—slide and pressed the intercom button. "April?"

"Yeah, Mom," her fourteen-year-old daughter's winded voice rang out. Kimberly grimaced. She must have been doing a cheerleader routine instead of her homework. During the spring, April took cheerleading at a dance studio and participated in competitions. In the fall she cheered at school, but she was supposed to be doing her homework.

"Can you come to the kitchen to help out?"

"I'll be there in a minute."

Kimberly called her son, who thought he was nearly grown at sixteen, and beckoned his assistance, too, then smiled and turned the sizzling chicken over in the pan. Since picking up her daughter from cheerleading, she'd gotten a late start. In addition, her son's car was in the shop for a recall, forcing her to pick him up from baseball practice. If she were smart, she would have had dinner delivered.

In the distance, Kimberly heard a cell phone

ringing and the low timbre of Jack's voice as he climbed the stairs. A few minutes later Jack returned, but he'd changed into a navy polo shirt without the bar's logo.

"Honey, how much longer before dinner is ready?" he asked, frowning as he checked the contents in one of the pots. "I thought you said we could eat as soon as I got home." Jack glanced impatiently at the clock. "Dinner smells great, but I could have brought something with me if you were busy. You have to be halfway starved by now."

"You are hungry, aren't you? Well, it's almost ready."

"What can I do to help?" he asked, just as the kids thundered in the kitchen. Their smiles brightened when they saw their father.

This was a good plan, Kimberly knew, even though dinner *was* a little late. At least they were all together for a change.

Jack helped the kids set the table as she dished the food on platters. When they sat around the table, Jack said grace, and Kimberly felt a degree of contentment. They had their problems, but this was the first step in working them out. They'd have the evening together, and she and Jack would talk—among other things. Warmth and desire spread through Kimberly.

But as soon as she opened her eyes, Jack was quickly shoveling food on his plate, and not very much of it. It was his favorite meal. Did he eat before he came home? Kimberly wondered, as she slowly filled her own plate.

Before she could take two bites, Jack was pushing back from the table. "Dinner was delicious," he said, wiping his mouth with the napkin.

They hadn't had time to share a conversation with the kids. "Where are you going?" Kimberly asked, puzzled by his actions.

"I'm sorry, honey, but I have to go back to work. I have a meeting I can't get out of." He headed to the door. "See you later, guys."

Tossing her napkin on the table, Kimberly got up and followed him, shutting the garage door after her so the children wouldn't overhear their conversation.

"You said you were going to spend the evening at home," Kimberly said. "We rarely see you anymore."

"I only planned to stay for a little while." With keys in hand, he used the remote to unlock the car door.

Kimberly had been running on all barrels all day. Jack's impending departure brought to the fore the tiredness that had waited to suck her under.

"You've only been here a half hour, if that much."

"I thought food would be ready when I got here, then we could have spent the entire time together." Jack sighed. "Honey, I keep telling you you can't do everything. Working full-time isn't working out."

"Let's not start on that again. I love my job—and this has nothing to do with my schedule."

"Then at least hire full-time help."

"I want us to be a regular family."

Jack massaged his temple. "We aren't a regular family. We barely have any time together. I've been saying that for months. I miss the mornings we used to spend making love after the children left for school."

"If you came home early sometimes, we could spend some evenings together."

"I run five brewpubs. My busiest times are the evenings."

"You hire managers to run them," Kimberly said, repeating herself like an old, scratched record. "You hired an assistant to help you. Let her relieve you some evenings."

"Kim, I don't have time to argue tonight. I'm late as it is."

Jack activated the remote to raise the garage door and then settled in the car. Slowly, Kimberly went inside the house and sat at the table with her children.

"Mama, dinner is good," April said.

"Thanks, honey." Kimberly noticed her son was watching her, and she smiled even though she felt like crying.

She and Jack couldn't go on this way. They shared very little these days. It was as if they shared the same roof but lived separate lives.

Weekdays, Kimberly was on the air at 5:00 a.m. with the first edition of the weather. She had to leave the house at three, so it wasn't as if she could spend half the night waiting for Jack to come in. More often lately, he'd come in long after she'd gone to bed.

Kimberly couldn't eat very much. The food could have been cardboard, for all she tasted. April had lost her appetite, too, but she forced down half of what was on her plate. Byron attacked his like a human garbage disposal. Nothing interfered with his appetite. As thin as he was, she didn't know where it all went, and he seemed always ready for more.

Already, Byron stood eye-to-eye with Jack, and April had his dimples on her cheeks and his pretty eyes. Jack hated for her to describe his brown eyes as pretty, but they were.

Kimberly asked the kids questions about school and their friends, and they answered in their usual disinterested fashion. But she kept talking until they became engaged in the conversation.

"Mom, I want to go to cheerleader camp this summer. It's only a week. It's someplace in Pennsylvania, only a six-hour drive from here. You can take me."

"I don't know. You're spending a couple of weeks with your uncle in the Caribbean, a week on a college campus for that science camp, and another week with my mother. As it is, I have to schedule time to get to see my own daughter. Do you think you'll have time for cheerleader camp, too?"

"I don't know, but I need to go."

"We'll see."

And Jack wanted her to quit her job. The kids were already out of the house most of the time.

They launched into a discussion about Byron's summer schedule, none of which included time with dear old mom.

Jack wanted Kimberly to hire a full-time person around the house, but although the place was enormous, she liked having privacy, having a one-on-one relationship with her children, and she loved to cook.

Stacking a few dishes in the dishwasher wasn't that big a deal. She hired a cleaning service for twice a week and felt that was enough.

After dinner, Kimberly sent the children to finish their homework, and after cleaning up the kitchen she showered, spread on face cream and then rubbed her favorite scented lotion all over her body. Today was one of those days when she felt every one of her thirty-five years.

Lately, Jack had complained a lot about her absences and their lack of time together. He complained more bitterly about the lack of sex. Men got crazy when they went without for too long. They hadn't had much of a relationship lately. And truth be told, she missed their lovemaking, too.

Kimberly remembered the little surprises she used to plan for Jack when they were younger. Jack's sister would babysit so they could have some time alone together. When was the last time she and Jack had gone out on a date? Of course he would blame her working hours for that, as well. Weekends were his busy time, but a couple of months ago he hired an assistant to take up some of the slack. The woman should be working most of the weekends by now.

The problem was that Jack was too controlling. But Jack visited each pub sometime over the weekend, often in connection with a business meeting, or just dinner or drinks with friends, or business associates and his suppliers. He should let his managers do their jobs and run the brewpubs. They were all well qualified. She'd pointed that out to him several times, but he never listened to her.

* * *

Jack felt restless. He didn't know why he was so discombobulated lately. Home life was falling apart. He'd attacked Kimberly unfairly, but seeing her in her jeans and T-shirt, her hair gathered in a ponytail, just set him off.

What happened to the time she'd let her hair hang loose, shiny and full? Kimberly knew how to dress to tempt him without being obvious or lewd. The kids were clueless to the simmering sexual tension between the adults. He remembered her wearing lounging wear that seemed perfectly chaste and sedate, but clung loosely to her curves, tempting him, because he knew the softness of her skin beneath. Her sensual movements and smiles seduced him. Jack shook his head. He couldn't wait for them to close their bedroom door and cling to each other.

Now she was fast asleep when he got home.

To top that, dinner wasn't ready, and he had to meet with Lauren Dorsey soon.

He realized Kimberly ran after the kids with a million after-school projects. She was a good mother, but… Damn it, he wanted a wife. Was that asking for too much?

He sighed and drove to the brewpub closest to where they lived. Lauren was waiting for him on the sidewalk.

The truth was, he felt guilty about checking out a bar with Lauren. Guilty because Kimberly didn't want him to open another brewpub. She was always complaining about his hours. But he was a businessman, and although she owned a half interest in the pubs, she hadn't worked with him in more than ten years. She'd pitched in to help the first few years, but after they purchased the second one, she began to get more involved with her own work.

But any business must grow or die. Didn't she understand that?

A new bar had gone on the market. The man who owned and ran the place for decades had passed away and his nieces and nephews wanted to sell it and split the profits. One of the nephews had approached Jack.

"You're early," Lauren Dorsey said, sliding into the seat. She wore a pair of black slacks with a matching blouse and a beige jacket. "I thought we were going to check out the place later on."

"Change of plans. We'll have dinner there, get a feel for their customer base."

Lauren placed her huge purse on the floor by her feet. At thirty-three, she was at least five-seven to Kimberly's five-five. Lauren had shoulder-length brown hair, unlike his wife's, which was a rich shade of midnight black. Most black hair actually contained hues of brown, but not Kimberly's. He loved to see it hanging loose down her back, and run his fingers through the long, silky strands. He compressed his lips in irritation. Another treat he was denied of late. By the time he made it home she had it all rolled up and a scarf tied on her head. Was this how life and marriage was supposed to be?

Jack thought of his father. How had his parents made it without fights like this? He didn't remember that his father wasn't there for dinner. He knew how hard his father worked. His picture of how a family worked was before his father died. As a child, it seemed easier somehow. Dinner was always ready. Everything ran smoothly; but then, his mother didn't work outside the home.

Trying to shake his irritation with his marriage, he maneuvered the car into the traffic.

It was the tail end of rush hour, and the traffic around the Beltway toward Prince George's County was still heavy, although the speed was decent. Jack was lucky, because Beltway traffic could easily become a crawl.

"I'm very excited about being in on the beginning of an acquisition," Lauren said. "I think it's a good idea to expand in this area."

Jack tore his concentration from thoughts of Kimberly. "The timing is right. The surrounding neighborhood has older homes. Singles and couples in their late twenties and thirties are buying fixeruppers as the older residents die off. From what I can tell, the younger crowd doesn't like to hang out at that bar." Jack wished he was sharing this with Kimberly. He wished she appreciated what he was trying to do. Maybe then she wouldn't try to put limitations on him.

When they arrived, Jack noticed only a few cars in the parking lot, but more people were inside than he expected. There was a handful of booths, all full but one. Most of the small tables were empty, but the bar was huge, and several people, mostly serious drinkers, sat and nursed drinks. They probably lived in the neighborhood and walked to the bar.

Jack and Lauren made their way to the only available booth. He leaned toward Lauren.

"He also owned the vacant store next door. That space, and the apartment in back, will open this space up to a decent-size pub," Jack said, as he plucked frayed plastic menus from between the salt and pepper shakers and handed one to Lauren. He wanted to get a feel for the menu, and the customer base—what appealed to customers in the area. Most of all, he needed to determine a plan that would pull in the younger thirtysomething groups.

Fried pork chops was the special of the day. At least they served Buffalo wings as one of the appetizers. The menu was limited, and although the bar was pretty crowded, it was an older crowd. They needed a more varied selection of food.

The local news, mostly ignored, blared from the one TV behind the bar. Old, scarred furniture was polished to a shine. Though it was well maintained, it was glaringly apparent that no one had updated the building or the fixtures in a couple of decades. There weren't enough TVs, so that patrons could also watch a game while they chatted with friends.

Jack liked the neighborhood. Condos and office buildings were nearby—a great customer base. Adrenaline pumped at the thought of opening a new establishment and turning it into a great place where people could meet and eat. There was something fresh, invigorating and hopeful about creating something new. He wanted this place. Deep down in his gut, he really wanted this place. But how was he going to convince his wife? In no uncertain terms, Kimberly had asked him not to open another brewpub.

Jack sighed. He'd just run the numbers, see if he could afford it. That wasn't buying it, was it?

Jack and Lauren had eaten appetizers and nursed a drink as they studied customers coming and going. After two hours, they left for one of his bars.

Jack's Place was huge, with an oblong-shaped granite and copper bar. Every stool on every side was occupied. Ten TVs placed strategically allowed customers to watch from almost anywhere in the room. Big copper vessels, kettles and tubing for brewing his own special brands of beer were always an attractive crowd-pleaser. His customers came in for the experience as much as for the food and drinks. The place to meet with friends or make new friends. The longer they stayed, the more they ordered appetizers with their drinks. Huge windows and an outside eating area were also available and always full this time of year.

Inside, a group of women beckoned to Jack. Dressed in a variety of outfits from jeans and short-sleeve sweater blouses to suits, some of them hadn't even made it home yet. High heels displayed fine-looking legs. He should be way past the lure, but he was still a man, and he wasn't blind to the appeal of an attractive woman. He wasn't attracted to any of these women, but he loved the energy of the pub.

He never forgot he was married. He could look, but he wouldn't touch. After all was said and done, he loved Kimberly. She was his one and only. And the truth was, he'd like to look at *her* in a pair of heels. He'd like to see *her* legs in a skirt. She used to greet him in sexy little outfits, or surprise him. That stopped years ago. She had a pair of fine-looking legs that he rarely got a chance to see, unless she was on the run to the car to drive the children somewhere.

As the host and owner, he joined the women and joked with them for a couple of minutes before he left for the back room to discuss the new project with Lauren.

Two hours later he went home. Kimberly was fast asleep, but a subtle scent of her perfume still lingered. There was a time he'd snuggle her in his arms. Jack sighed and slid between the sheets. To his annoyance, he wasn't even in the mood to hold her tonight.

The truth was, he felt stifled—and guilt weighed heavily on his conscience for making plans to open another brewpub against Kimberly's wishes. He could tell himself a thousand times that he was just running the numbers, but he knew if everything clicked, he'd want to buy. And he'd have the fight of his life with his wife.

His dream was to have his brewpubs as well-known as Budweiser beer. He'd started with the D.C. metro area. He wanted to open five more pubs in the next two years and then begin to spread out. He'd socked away enough money to begin to grow.

A terrible weight settled on Jack's chest. Would fulfilling his dream mean he'd have to lose the woman he loved? Would he have to give up his goals to keep Kimberly? Was it fair for him to pursue his desires and force her to give up hers? One of them needed to be home with the children. His mother was always home with them, until his stepfather wiped them out.

Jack knew he was acting like a jerk, but this was more than dreams, it was security. More than anything, kids needed the security of a roof over their heads and to know that money for college was a given. He knew. He knew what it was like to go without. There was a time he thought he wouldn't be able to attend college, that he'd have to get a full-time job to help his mother pay bills. But the housing market did well, and his mother worked hard as a real estate agent. By the time he left for college, she was making enough to manage the household.

When his stepfather left, Jack had to work nights and weekends, spending the rest of the night studying to keep his grades up. Because, now that his college money was gone, he needed a scholarship to attend the college of his dreams.

But his kids weren't babies any longer. Byron would be gone in a couple of years and April soon after. He and Kimberly were still young enough to pursue dreams. But at this age, if at least one parent didn't stay immersed in the children's lives, they'd find all kinds of trouble to get into. He was there for them in the mornings, made an effort to talk to them— but Kimberly thought that wasn't enough.

Smothering an oath, Jack gathered Kimberly into his arms. She smelled sweet and he wanted to make love.

But she needed her rest.

Resigning himself, he dozed off to sleep.

* * *

The next morning, Jack prepared breakfast for the kids while the low drone of the TV sounded in the background. Every Sunday, Kimberly attached the week's breakfast menu to the fridge with a magnet. Friday was pancakes.

She believed in homemade stuff, so he added the wet ingredients to the mix she'd already prepared. It was easy enough to do, and if the kids complained, he always told them to complain to their mother.

The aroma drifted up the stairs, bringing April to the kitchen. With her eyes puffy, she looked as if she'd barely slept all night. At least she'd dressed decently. For a while, they'd had arguments about her wearing too-skimpy clothes for his tastes. She'd called him ancient, but this was his baby and she wasn't leaving the house looking like she was headed to a street corner.

With long black hair and a face quickly maturing to be a real beauty, she was almost a carbon copy of her mother, and growing up way too fast to suit him.

"You've got to stay off that computer at night," he told her, chucking her under the chin. "If it happens again, I'm taking it out of your room."

She slid into a seat at the table. "I wasn't on the computer." Her lips actually trembled.

"What's wrong, baby?" Concerned, he pulled out a chair beside her and sat.

Heavy lashes shadowing her cheeks flew up. "Are you and Mama getting a divorce?"

"Of course not," he said, surprised she'd jumped to

that conclusion over a simple disagreement. "What made you think that?"

"Most of my friends' parents are already divorced or getting one." Her concerned eyes met his. "And you were fighting. You don't usually fight. This felt different. Daddy, I don't want a stepfather." Her voice cracked on the last word and her lips trembled.

The thought of Kimberly in the arms of another man sent panic through Jack. She wouldn't leave him simply because he was opening another pub, would she?

"Just because we were arguing, it doesn't mean we're getting a divorce." He tweaked April's nose, hoping to bring her out of her melancholy. "You and your brother fight all the time, but nobody's moving out. You're still digging in my wallet. I can see some shopping coming up." He'd meant to get a smile out of her, but it wasn't working.

"That's how it starts. When my friends' parents started fighting and staying apart, the next thing they knew, their dad was moving out. Then their parents started fighting for sure, and seeing lawyers for a divorce."

"Tell you what. I'm going to see if your mom can get a few days off so I can take her on a little vacation. Just the two of us. We're just fine," he said, trying to cheer her up. But he knew things weren't fine. And he didn't have only himself to consider. He had two children who needed both their parents.

"See, you lost all that sleep for nothing," he said. "Eat your food. I'll even spring for whipped cream, strawberries and powdered sugar. Just don't tell your mama about the extra sugar." He tapped her on the tip of her nose—a nose that looked so much like her mother's. April's sunny smile finally burst free, and his worry diminished.

Kimberly's animated voice on the tube captured their attention, and their gazes riveted to her as she gave the weather report.

"We won't see any rain in the next five days," she said. "A lovely weekend for outdoor activities."

Kimberly enjoys her job and is a natural on camera, Jack thought, and he felt guilty about asking her to quit it or cut back on hours, especially since he couldn't cut back on his.

It left him in such a quandary.

He focused on her again.

"What's the traffic pattern around town, Bob?"

When the camera switched back to Bob Hartman, Jack got up to pile pancakes on a plate for April. She was always conscious of diet, but he cajoled her into eating some of it anyway. Otherwise the child would turn into an anorexic.

His and Kimberly's seventeenth anniversary was coming up. They needed to get away for a few days. Not a whole week, but he could spare a little time.

He left a voice mail on Kimberly's cell, asking if she could take a couple of days off next week. They'd fly to the Caribbean. His kids were his mother's only grandchildren. Knowing she would be more than happy to spend a few days with them, he called her to set it up.

* * *

With a stack of papers in his hand that he intended to take upstairs to his corporate office on the second floor, Jack went to the bar to tell the new bartender not to take any more drink orders. The eight people who worked there left hours ago. It was nearly two and the place was almost cleared out.

At the bar, he saw one damn good-looking sista sitting by her lonesome. He came around the end of the bar so he could get a good look at her.

Have mercy. He felt punched in the gut.

A woman out alone at night when the place was closing in two minutes was looking for something.

She wore a black, sleeveless dress, the hem of which had slid halfway up her thigh. Slowly and seductively, his gaze started at the stilettos, the toe of which hung on the chair rung. It worked its way up the greatest pair of legs he'd ever laid eyes on. He kept going north until he collided with the hem of her skirt. Didn't she know what shoes and legs like that did to a man?

But the legs weren't all she was blessed with. She was well endowed, but not overly so, he thought, as the material molded around a generous pair of breasts. She was classy. Even as he gazed at her, her nipples peaked against the fabric and his body immediately responded by tightening against the zipper of his pants. Good thing his shirttail was out and hung down past his hips.

This woman knew he was watching and he knew she wasn't immune to him.

Her left hand was wrapped around a glass. She was

dripping in diamonds and didn't even try to hide the huge engagement ring or the platinum wedding band studded with more diamonds. There should be a law against husbands letting their wives out alone at night dressed like that.

His employees were cleaning, trying to leave as soon as they could.

"Bartender, may I have a refill?" the woman asked the man behind the bar.

"I'm sorry, ma'am, the bar is closed."

Unable to stop himself, Jack dropped his papers on the bar and approached her.

"Give her a refill, Stan. On me," he said.

For the first time, her gaze met his for a brief second—before she stared into her empty glass. "Thank you," she said sweetly.

"Is this seat taken?" Jack asked.

"No," she said. Her voice was husky and she cleared her throat.

"Mind if I join you?"

"How can I refuse after you so kindly bought my drink?"

He eased himself into the swivel seat and turned so he could gaze at her. "I know it's a sad cliché, but what's a fine-looking sista like you doing in a place like this alone?"

"You ask a lot of questions," she said.

He tapped the diamond. "Does Mr....?"

She did not fill in the blank, so Jack tapped her ring with his forefinger and continued. "Does he mind your being out with another man?"

"I'm alone," she said, smiling seductively.

Jack smiled. "Not any longer." Something intense flared through him. How long had it been since he'd played this game?

Too long.

The bartender placed the drink in front of her and took her empty glass.

She took an experimental sip. "One drink only entitles you to one question. You're already over your quota. Let me ask *you* a question." Her eyes, dreamy eyes, lit on his.

"Shoot." Jack crossed his arms over his chest and settled in to enjoy himself.

"Why are you still here if the bar is closed?"

Jack leaned back in his seat. "I'm the owner. I can stay as long as I want."

Her eyes lit up with interest. "You're the famous Jack Canter I read about in the paper?"

"I don't know about being famous."

"I read that you're married and have two children."

"And?"

"Is there a problem?" the woman asked.

"I'm done here," the bartender said, breaking into their conversation. "Can I get you anything else before I go?"

Jack never took his eyes off the woman. "I can handle it from here. Just leave the one light on and lock the doors when you leave."

Stan raised his eyebrows and gave them a look, then nodded and disappeared without another word.

"My office is more comfortable," Jack said. "May I take you there?"

"Do you always invite strange women into your office?" Kimberly laughed.

Jack shook his head, enjoying the game. "Never. But you don't exactly fit that mold. Anyway—" he smiled again "—I'm not forcing you. It's up to you." He nodded to the door. "I'll even walk you to your car, if that's what you want."

She gathered up her black, designer purse, took her drink and followed him.

How many times had he fantasized about being with Kimberly like this?

She smiled as he took her arm and led her through the door that lead to a short corridor. There, the stairs led to a set of offices. He watched those sexy legs as he slowed his step so she could walk in front of him. The sway of her hips as she ascended the stairs played havoc with his libido. Upstairs, he opened the door for her.

Pushed against one wall was a sleeper sofa that doubled as a bed when the weather turned foul and he spent the night. There was always fresh linen on it, but he didn't open it.

He gazed at her closely. He'd like to take his time and make love to her for hours, but he knew their time was limited. They were there for one reason and one reason only. There would be no tomorrow, only tonight. Jack felt wicked, and a burst of excitement quickened his heartbeat.

There was a fridge in his office filled with bottles of wine and beer. He took out a bottle that was recently brewed and opened it, all the while very aware that she was there waiting for him.

"May I get you a glass of wine?" he asked. A delightful shiver of desire ran through him.

"No. I'm fine," she said.

"You are that," he agreed and he screwed off the top and took a long swallow.

She blushed and turned to the desk, placing her purse and drink there. She spotted the photos and nodded toward them. "Your wife and kids?"

"Yes." He nodded.

"Nice family," Kimberly said with amusement.

"I think so," he murmured in agreement, still enjoying the game.

"Then why am I here?"

"Because I want you and I hope you want me, too." He moved the bottle to his lips and took a long drink.

She seemed mesmerized as he swallowed and placed the bottle on the desk, before his gaze landed on her.

She turned her back to him and he eased up behind her. Lifting her heavy hair aside, he kissed her on the neck. With a sweet moan, her neck rolled to the side to give him better access.

He reasoned that they should be getting home, that after this fantasy played out, he and Kimberly had a lot to work through. *But none of that's going to stop me from sampling her,* he thought, as he caressed her shoulders and eased the zipper down her long back, hoping he wasn't moving too fast, knowing he couldn't stop.

Kimberly didn't play these kinds of sex games often. The dress slid from her shoulders and he reached around and unhooked the front clasp of her bra and eased the straps down her arms, enjoying the smoothness of her skin.

He wanted to take all night to make love to her, but neither of them had that long. And her moan forced him to move along. She smelled sweet, and he ran his fingers through her soft hair, lifting it to the other side to give him access to her long neck.

His body hardened and he rubbed against her back.

A delicious shudder heated her body, and she reached back, gathering his hard erection in her hand, caressing him through his slacks.

He groaned out loud and turned her in his arms. The heat coming from his eyes was intense with need. He kissed the corner of her mouth, then moved his lips softly across her lips, back and forth. But she ached for more. She slid her hands around his back, enjoying the feel of his muscles against her fingertips. As he kissed her, his hands roamed over her hot, curvy body.

He cupped Kimberly's behind, massaged her cheeks and drew her close, pressing her breasts against his chest. They moved against him with need. He was taking too long. She pressed her tongue against the seam of his lips and he opened to her immediately, and all but devoured her.

"Damn, baby, you're ready for me, aren't you?" he whispered before he captured her mouth in a breath-stealing kiss that wiped her mind of everything but him. He took his time kissing her, until it wasn't enough.

"You taste sweet," he said and she moaned again.

His arousal was pressed hard against her stomach, but she didn't seem to notice as her hands clawed at his back, lifting the shirt up to touch his bare skin.

"Oh, baby, you're driving me crazy," he said, pushing the dress aside and kissing her on the shoulder, smoothing kisses across the top of her breasts, before he gathered those full orbs in his hands and lightly massaged them. "A lovely handful. So smooth. So soft. So beautiful," he whispered, his voice thick with need. He worked her nipple with his lips, then tugged lightly with his teeth until she was begging for more.

Her hands played his body like an instrument, striking all the right notes.

He pushed her back on the couch, pushed her legs open wide and kneeled before...and his startled eyes looked at her.

She wore no panties or thong. He kissed her inner thigh, teasing her with nipping little kisses, as if he could feast there the entire meal, nearing her center but not quite there.

"You're driving me crazy," she said in that sexy, husky, needful voice.

"I want you crazy for me," he said, in such a low and sexy voice it felt like a cool stroke down her spine.

And then he touched the heat of her desire and she cried out in pleasure, her butt jerking off the sofa.

"Oh, Jack...that feels so good," she cried out, digging her fingers into his shoulders.

"Oh, baby. So sweet. So beautiful."

She whimpered senseless words of encouragement, of need, as he played her like a skilled musician, tearing cries of pleasure from her. Her thoughts fragmented as his hands and lips continued their hungry exploration of her body, until she began to vibrate with liquid fire. A tremor heated her until great gulps of desire shook her. And then the orgasm rocked through her, sending pleasure to every point of her body.

Jack's erection was thick and heavy when he adjusted her hips and entered her, until she was stretched and filled.

"It's been too damn long," he said in a ragged breath.

She wrapped her legs tightly around him, kissed him on the chest and he slid into her even deeper. He grabbed her butt cheeks and they moved to their own sweet rhythm.

The connection was tight and exquisite. Her heartbeat pounded in her chest. She was gasping for breath.

The tension increased until an orgasm hit her again and spread out, enveloping her whole body. Close behind, his guttural voice rang out in a husky, hoarse shout.

He stayed in that position until their breathing slowly subsided and he shifted his weight to the side, spooning her beside him, waiting for their heartbeats to calm. He made lazy circles on her breasts and stomach.

"Do you have to get home now?" he asked, placing a sweet kiss behind her ear as desire began to stir again.

"No. April is at a sleepover."

"Umm."

He nuzzled her neck, bit lightly on her earlobe. "So when the kids are away, hubby lets you out to play?"

She groaned as his tongue played out patterns on her neck. "Yes…"

"How generous of him. If you were my wife, I'd keep you in bed until they returned."

She laughed a full-throated sound, then groaned in delight as his fingers stroked her pleasure points.

"What century did you come from?"

"Does it matter?" he asked, sliding his hand down her thigh.

Desire curled in her center. "Not when you're making moves like that."

"Lots of women could take lessons from you."

"Is that right?"

"Maybe we should go. I'm hungry."

"Then you can heat up leftovers when we get home." The amiable tone of her voice was clearly gone.

He realized that her being here tonight was her way of trying to move past their argument, but that she was still sensitive about it. Better to keep this fragile closeness they had found.

He groaned, sliding his hands to her breasts, stroking her nipples. "I'm sorry, baby. I was in a bad mood yesterday. I'd gladly eat leftovers."

He turned her in his arms. "Let's kiss and make up."

Before they could move they heard footfalls on the stairs. "Shit," Jack said and hopped off her to grab his pants and pull them on. They'd left the door wide-open. He shut and locked it just before the intruder made it to the top.

"Jack? Are you in there?" Lauren's hesitant voice asked from the head of the stairs.

"Yeah, give me a moment," he said. "I'll be right out."

"What is she doing here this time of night?" Kimberly asked suspiciously.

Jack shrugged. "I don't know. She worked at the pub in D.C. tonight."

Kimberly ran a hand across her face. Their fantasy had been nice, for as long as it lasted. It was time to get back to reality.

Jack had already shrugged into his shirt and was zipping up his pants.

"We better get home," Kimberly said. She didn't want to act the suspicious wife, but Lauren's presence worried her. "So why do you think Lauren's here?"

"Beats me. I'll find out." Jack leaned down, kissed her sweetly on the lips. "Thanks for the present," he said. "When we get home, we'll pick up where we left off."

"I'm looking forward to it," she responded, forcing herself not to take the time to run her hands over his hard body.

"By the way—the message I left for you today…? We've got an anniversary coming up. Can you schedule a couple of days off? We can spend it on the island." They always called Canter Island, the island they owned with his brothers and sisters, "the island."

"I'd love to," she said excitedly, dragging his head down for a long kiss before she disappeared into his private bath. He still took her breath away, just as he had in college, when they'd first met—and before the year was up, she'd gotten pregnant. He was the only man she'd ever slept with, but she often wondered if he regretted having to marry her.

Yes, he wanted her to quit her job or work fewer hours, but she didn't want to give up her job completely. She felt that despite her love for her family, she still needed something that was completely hers. She worried that she'd lose herself if she didn't. The kids would be out of the house much too soon, and Jack was really dissatisfied with their marriage. Although she'd enjoyed their lovemaking, Kimberly knew great sex didn't cure anything.

From the moment she met Jack, she'd fallen in love with him hard, and today she loved him even more; there was no question about that. She just didn't know if he felt the same way about her. And she didn't know that giving up her own career for his was the right solution.

She wasn't suspicious by nature, nor a weak-minded woman who needed constant affirmation. But she needed to know he loved her and wanted to be with her. She heard lowered voices in the hallway and footsteps moving away from the door.

Jack scoffed whenever Kimberly mentioned that his new assistant was infatuated with him—even accused her of being paranoid and jealous. Kimberly wasn't blind. Jack was a very attractive and wealthy man. He wasn't when they married, but they'd done well over the years. It wouldn't be the first time one of his female employees would have attempted to work her way up in the company by trying to seduce Jack. They'd gotten fired for their efforts, but she worried that there was always a first time.

Kimberly viewed their upcoming trip as encouragement.

And in the meantime, she was going to keep an eye on Lauren.

Chapter 2

"Where did you say you were going?" Jonas Sherwood, Kimberly's producer, asked Wednesday morning with a puzzled look on his face. A very attractive, dark-complexioned man who stood at five-ten, he always appeared a little too neat. He reminded her of Felix in *The Odd Couple* sometimes, the way he was always obsessive about ensuring that everything was on schedule and in place. He'd moved from San Francisco to begin working at their station two months ago.

Kimberly glanced up from the screen. "Canter Island, a private island in the Caribbean. Why?"

"There's some movement in the Atlantic," one of the other forecasters said, "but for now, it's not coming anywhere near where you'll be."

Kimberly studied the readout. "I saw it. Hurricane Brighton is so far out that it might peter out. And if it doesn't, more than likely, I'll be back here before it nears the island," she said, studying the screen. It was mid-May and the hurricanes were starting early this year. They came in cycles, and they were going through a bad cycle right now.

Kimberly finished her observations and prepared her forecast, along with what she was going to say before she recorded a weather announcement for a local radio station.

She listened to her tape and the producer pronounced it ready. How she loved her job, she thought, as she positioned herself for the first forecast of the morning.

"We have a sixty percent chance of rain later this afternoon," she began. "Potentially after rush hour." She stood in front of what appeared to the viewers to be a map, but was actually a blank wall. "Currently it's fifty-seven degrees at Reagan National Airport. The temperature will reach a comfortable seventy-two degrees this afternoon." She pointed out the different temperatures in the surrounding areas. "Down the road to the south…" Kimberly continued, warming up to her topic.

Between her regular broadcasts, live radio weather reports and constant checks on weather conditions, the morning passed quickly, and before she knew it, she was on her way out the door.

"I have your cell number, if anything turns up," Jonas said. "Have a wonderful vacation. See you Monday." He focused on the screen again.

Kimberly had just enough time to get her hair done before she picked up April. She and Jack were taking the six-thirty flight out, but Kimberly still had a thousand chores before then. On her way to the hair-dresser's, her mother called.

"I wanted to wish you a happy anniversary before you left," Nona Boswell said in her usual, chipper voice.

"Thank you. I'm looking forward to getting away."

"How is Jack?"

"He's fine."

"Are you sure?" her mother inquired. "I've heard you all are fighting quite a bit."

April. Kimberly was going to muzzle her daughter. "We're fine. Jack's on a tear because I'm working full-time and we rarely see each other."

"Honey, most women work full-time."

"I know."

"I believe husbands and wives should work together to solve their differences. You're an intelligent woman. You know what to do to protect yourself and not be blindsided the way I was. Listen to your gut feelings. I was glad I was well established in my career when your dad left me. At least I could support myself, had good benefits and had built up my leave. Don't get me wrong. I like Jack a lot. But God gave women a brain for a reason."

"We aren't talking divorce, Mom."

"I know," Nona soothed. "But women have to protect themselves."

Kimberly doubted her mother dated very much

since her father left sixteen years ago. The monumental problem was that it was so hard for women to find suitable dates.

"You should consider moving to this area, now that you're retired," Kimberly said.

"My supervisor has asked me to come back and work part-time. They've had to hire two people to do my job and they're still understaffed. I know my job, and I can fill in for many of the others."

"Are you considering it?" Kimberly asked. "If you need extra money…"

"Honey, I can support myself. Why do you think I worked all those years? A couple days a week isn't bad, and it would keep me active. I hate sitting around," she said. "It's true there are lots of volunteer projects I could get involved with, but the extra income will help. I told them I'll start in October."

"They'll wait that long?"

"Yes. I'm going to travel this summer."

"Where are you going?" Kimberly asked, getting into her car. She was soon on her way.

"I'll spend a week on your island, but I'm thinking of Africa and China. I'll be away August and September…" Her mother continued to describe all the wonderful trips she'd planned.

Kimberly wondered if she and Jack would ever be able to get away to travel the way her mother did. So far, it had only been a week here and there. With jobs and children, taking vacations alone together had been impossible. Kimberly could schedule a leave, but Jack hated to stay away from the brewpubs for any length of time. They were doing very well to get away for this vacation.

"Who are you going with?" Kimberly asked.

She paused. "A friend."

"Do I know her?" Kimberly didn't miss the hesitation in her mother's voice. "What's her name?"

"*His* name is Frank."

A wry smile curved Kimberly's lips. "Is this a significant other?"

"Yes."

"When do I meet him?"

"I don't know."

"Is he a secret?" Kimberly asked suspiciously, wondering why her mother was so furtive. Pulling information was like pulling teeth.

Nona's sigh was drawn out. "He's white. And I don't know how you'll feel about that."

"Is he nice to you?"

"Very."

"And you like him?" Kimberly asked, already knowing the answer. Her mother wouldn't give the time of day to a man who didn't appeal to her.

"Yes."

"Of course I'm okay. I don't want you to be alone, when you can find someone nice to spend your time with."

"Your open-mindedness is a load off my chest."

"Mom, I worried about you being alone."

"I can take care of myself."

"My concern is more than financial. You need someone special in your life, too."

"I can't deny I've missed the intimacy. You wouldn't believe the losers I've dated. It's not easy. I thought I'd never find someone who would click with me. If I hadn't gone through all the drama, I don't think my heart would have been open to Frank. I would have preferred a black man. But we fell for each other, and I wasn't about to let the fact that he was a different race interfere."

"I'm glad."

Kimberly was ecstatic for her mother. Her father had left Nona soon after Kimberly and Jack married. The new woman was fifteen years younger than he, and he married her soon after the divorce was final. Her mother had been single and alone all these years. Part of the problem was that her mother had loved her husband. But Nona was proof positive that love didn't always stop the ceiling from caving in on you.

"I'll see you soon. Have a wonderful trip."

"Love you, Mom," Kimberly said. They disconnected just as she drove up to the apartment building where her hair salon was located.

After her appointment, Kimberly picked up her daughter from school. Minutes later, she entered their quiet Potomac, Maryland, neighborhood of stately homes, manicured lawns, pristine pools and luxury cars.

It wasn't uncommon for children to have an entire floor to themselves, and although they had the space, Kimberly drew the line at living separately from her children. With four bedroom suites on their floor, the kids didn't need to be on the third floor. It sat empty, except when April or Byron had sleepovers.

Kimberly didn't see the sense in having a house that large, but Jack was determined to acquire the best. There were three bedrooms on the third floor and a home office on the first floor.

At least it kept the cleaning service happy.

April was tapping her fingers to the beat of her music as Kimberly wheeled into the driveway and activated the remote for the garage door. April seemed much happier lately.

"Your grandmother should be here soon," Kimberly said, meaning Jack's mother, not hers.

"I know. I talked to her yesterday," April said, twisting in the seat. "I wanted to make sure she fixed all my favorite foods."

"April…"

"I'm her only granddaughter. She doesn't mind."

Kimberly shook her head. "You make sure you follow the rules while we're away. And don't work your grandmother so hard."

"Mom, you worry about everything. I'm not a baby anymore."

"That's what worries me," Kimberly said as her cell phone chimed.

It was Jack this time.

"I'm running a little late. The bags are already by the front door. Have the driver pick me up here."

"You aren't going to be late leaving, are you?" Kimberly asked suspiciously. The last time they planned a trip, Jack was so late they missed the flight.

"No. I'll be on time."

"What about your car?"

"I'll make arrangements to have it driven to the house."

"I'm leaving here in an hour," Kimberly said, making a mental note of last-minute chores.

"See you soon, honey."

Truth be told, Kimberly was looking forward to this vacation. She hated leaving her children, but they'd be in good hands with Jack's mother.

And Kimberly desperately wanted to reconnect with her husband.

As soon as they were in the air, Jack pulled out his business papers. But this was supposed to be an anniversary trip—not an off-site meeting. Unwilling to start the trip with a fight, Kimberly felt okay with napping instead of trying to stir up a conversation. At least they were in first class and not scrunched up like cattle being herded to market. It had been so long since Kimberly had had one-on-one time with her husband that she didn't know what they'd do together, except for the obvious. Perhaps they could use this as an opportunity to bond.

Sex was never the problem.

It was outside the bedroom that they didn't mesh anymore.

When they landed at the minuscule island airport, they took a water taxi to Canter Island. Lights shimmered on the aquamarine water. Sailboats skipped along the surface of the water, while speedboats bobbed. The vegetation was lush and green, the fragrant flowers colorful.

When they reached the island, the night lights illuminated the profusion of flowers everywhere. A few of the workers lived on the island, but most of them came in from larger islands. The hotel was surrounded by ten cabanas situated among lush plants.

A friendly driver met them at the pier. "Good evening, Mr. and Mrs. Canter. It's a pleasure to have you with us."

"I'm pleased to be back," Jack said. "Is my brother around, or has he retired for the evening?"

"He's off-island. He's disappointed he couldn't meet you, but he'll return later tonight and will see you tomorrow. I'm sure you're tired after your flight," the driver said.

"That we are," Jack said.

All of the employees knew Jack well, due to his bimonthly trips to check on things since the hotel first opened. Now his brother managed the hotel, and Jack had stopped his visits to concentrate on expanding his brewpubs.

Once their bags were stowed in the back of the Jeep, they climbed in and were driven directly to the largest cabana. The driver opened the door and handed two key cards to Jack. After delivering the luggage, he left, quite satisfied with the tip Jack handed him.

The light and breezy ambience of the cabana on the beach immediately lifted Kimberly's spirits. The furniture was white, and there were pastel curtains.

"The first thing I want to do tomorrow is hit the beach." Kimberly yawned and unpacked her suitcase. She'd been up since two that morning. Now it was close to midnight. All she wanted was sleep. Since Jack appeared equally as tired, they went to bed. It was late morning before either of them awakened.

"Maybe we should grab a bite to eat," Jack said, after they showered and dressed.

"Let's get something from the bar on the beach." Kimberly smoothed sunblock over her body and regarded herself critically in the mirror. Her swimsuit was new. She'd brought it specifically to tantalize Jack. She was still in shape, thanks to trips to the gym three times a week. With being on TV, she couldn't afford to swell up. Not a woman.

Maybe she and Jack could find a way back to each other. The last time they'd made love had been hurried. And that had been a week ago. When had they done something simple, like holding hands while taking a leisurely walk? Or just cuddle the night away, watching old movies or listening to music? She even went to the theater with friends—but never with Jack. But he'd initiated this trip, so he must miss her as much as she missed him.

She gazed at herself again to make sure she looked sexy.

After tying a sarong around her waist, she joined Jack. He'd already changed into his trunks and was talking on the phone. She sighed. This was supposed to be their time together.

Okay, okay. She was going to put a positive spin on this. He owned businesses. He had to stay in touch.

He laughed, looking a lot more relaxed than he did before she went into the bathroom. Was she being paranoid?

"Okay, Lauren. See you when I get back." Still smiling, he hung up the phone.

Hearing Lauren's name immediately sapped Kimberly's good mood. "Ready?" she asked.

"Yeah."

Taking her cell phone out of her purse, she asked, "Did you call your mother?"

"No."

Kimberly dialed their number and talked to her mother-in-law for a few minutes. April had perked up considerably before they left. Even tucked a bottle of scented lotion into Kimberly's suitcase. After a brief conversation, Kimberly smiled and hung up.

When she turned around, Jack was stretched out on the bed sound asleep, even though they'd slept the night away. Kimberly started to awaken him, then changed her mind. Instead, she wrote a note telling him she was going to the beach. Disappointed, she grabbed her wide-brimmed hat and a thin, long-sleeve white cover-up and left the room. She worked mornings. Jack worked nights. She was accustomed to doing things on her own, but she hadn't planned on spending her second honeymoon alone. He could have his nap. They had the rest of the trip to be together.

An hour later, Jack awakened, disoriented. He remembered they were in the tropics. And he was starving. He rubbed his hand over his face.

"Kim," he called out to no response. Hefting himself off the bed, he went searching for her. She wasn't in the bathroom. He used the facilities, then brushed his teeth before he went back to the main room and saw the note on the dresser. He quickly read the terse message. She'd gone to the beach.

She would have eaten. He might as well order something light. They'd have dinner together. By then she would have calmed down. He didn't understand why she was so touchy lately. He couldn't say two words without her getting bent out of shape.

While he waited for room service, Jack pulled out his cell phone and made several calls. By the time he finished, the food had arrived. The news had spoiled his appetite.

There was another buyer interested in the bar. He had to work fast if he wanted a running chance at getting it, and there was no question that he wanted it.

While he ate, he opened his briefcase and spread papers on the desk. He could get some work done while he waited for Kim to return.

He paused a moment, a smidgen of guilt dragging at him. What did she expect him to do? Sit around and drink bourbon every day and not work? Shoot the breeze with the guys? It wasn't his nature. He couldn't have his son watching him live a life of leisure. The boy would think work wasn't a requirement, and for a man it was. He didn't want his daughter marrying a man unwilling to work to provide for his family. Children watched their parents.

Kimberly was going through one of her phases. Suddenly his heartbeat quickened. Could she be pregnant? Was that the reason she was acting so strange? The reason she wanted him home more? If that was the case, he needed to work harder than ever—if he had another mouth to provide for.

He realized that he hoped she *was* pregnant. They'd wanted another child, but after so long, they had finally quit trying.

He began to weigh the pros and cons of opening a new brewpub. If he even mentioned the idea to Kimberly, he could kiss any kind of pleasant times on this trip goodbye. She'd spend the entire time nagging him to change his mind.

Jack still hadn't come out to the beach. Kimberly had washed down a small serving of fried conch with a margarita. Later, she went into the cool, crystal-clear water for an hour. Several guys had already tried to pick her up, but she made it clear she was married.

She was going in soon. Perhaps Jack would be finished with his nap. She pulled herself out of the ocean and grabbed a towel to wipe off.

She heard a low whistle, and it took a lot to stop an eye roll.

"Hey, baby. Mind if I join you?" A tall, potbellied, medium-complexioned guy came strutting her way. He had to be in his midfifties at least. And she definitely *wasn't* his baby. "I'm with someone," she said and amended to herself, *she* should *be with her husband.* She turned her back to the man and hoped he had the good sense to go about his business.

"I've been watching you for hours, and I haven't seen anyone. If you were my woman, I wouldn't let you outta my sight. Don't play hard to get, baby. No sense in spending your vacation alone when Joe's on the scene."

She was about to give him a piece of her mind when she heard a familiar voice.

"Having a problem?" her brother-in-law asked, as he approached them. Devin and Jack were almost the same height. At thirty-six, Devin was two years younger.

"Am I?" she asked the man, quirking an eyebrow.

He shrugged and stalked off.

Devin eased his attractive form onto the lounger beside her and leaned back. "So where's my brother? He's got to be out of his mind to leave you alone on your second honeymoon."

"He was sleeping when I left the room."

"That's what you get for marrying an old man. Have you had lunch?"

"I had a snack earlier, but I'm going to order something light."

"Why don't we eat together? Beachside? Or would you prefer the dining room?"

"Beachside, I think. I'd have to change for the dining room. But you don't have to entertain me. I can take care of myself."

"Haven't seen you in a while. And I have to eat. I can't think of better company. Over lunch, you can tell me all about my niece and nephew and what everybody back home is up to. I'm looking forward to spending a couple of weeks with them this summer." There was a wistful look on his face.

Anytime someone spoke favorably about her children, Kimberly melted like butter. "You spoil them. They can't wait to get here. And once they return home, they talk about their visit the rest of the year."

"It's my job to spoil them."

"And your mother constantly complains that you don't call home enough. Shame on you."

Devin frowned. "Every time I call her we get into a conversation about marriage and her wanting to set me up with some friend's daughter. 'You know she's a good girl, because she's in church every Sunday,'" he mimicked. "She just won't leave it alone. And I'm tired of talking about it."

Devin had married three years ago. The wife he believed was so in love with him had actually married him for his money. He'd caught her with her true love when he came home from work early one day to surprise her. It was a surprise all right. She'd used the credit cards Devin had given her to buy the man expensive gifts. When he'd filed for divorce, she'd even tried to get half his assets, but Devin had a great attorney who hired a private investigator to do a background check. His wife got nothing.

Needless to say, Devin didn't believe in love any longer. Which was sad. He'd turned from the carefree, happy, hardworking man that he was, to a more cynical player. They'd discussed his actions, but he said he always let his dates know up front not to get serious about him, because he wasn't going to ever get involved in a serious relationship.

After the divorce, he let his sister take over manage-

ment of his company, while he came to the island to
manage the family property and to get away from it all.

"Are you happy here?" Kimberly asked softly,
studying his eyes for the truth.

"Who couldn't be happy, with warm breezes and
endless parties?" he said with finality. This topic was
definitely off-limits. "As a matter of fact, we're having
a beach party tonight. Bring the old man."

"We'll be there." She knew Devin was still hurt-
ing—still unable to trust.

Kimberly squeezed his hand, then settled back to sip
her drink while they waited for their food. He needed
a good woman. She shook her head. She was having
problems with her own marriage. What right did she
have, trying to fix up someone else?

After a sumptuous snack, Kimberly picked up her
things and made her way to the cabana.

Deeply engrossed in his work, Jack didn't even
hear her enter.

"Why didn't you join me at the beach?" she asked.
"Why did you come here, if all you were going to do
was work? We could have stayed home for that."

"I didn't come to work, but you were out, so I
decided to get a few things done."

"You knew where I was," Kimberly said, annoyed
that, while he was inside working, men were hitting on
her.

"I knew you'd be back soon." He sighed. "Let's not
start another fight, okay? I'm finished anyway. Let's
dress for dinner and have a lovely evening together."

Kimberly sincerely wanted an evening without

fighting—an evening getting close to each other again. The nap seemed to have revived him. He looked rested. "Did you have a good nap?"

"Oh, yeah."

He worked much too hard. He needed some time off for himself.

"I'll agree, if you forget about work for the rest of the vacation."

He came over, gathered her into his arms. "Hmm. You smell warm and taste of salt." He nipped her shoulder. "I love the way you taste, baby."

Kimberly moaned and curved her arms around him, feeling his familiar strength before she kissed him full on the mouth. She loved him. She didn't want to fight. Her heart skipped a beat. She loved him so very much. He was like a seductive drug in her veins. Her deepest worry had been what she would do if they couldn't find a way back to each other.

There was a way. She just had to search for it.

Jack patted her on the backside and eased from her. "Let's get ready for dinner."

"What are you working on?" Kimberly asked, when she saw papers scattered on the desk.

"I thought we were going to forget about business while we're here," he replied.

"It was important enough for you to bring, it's important enough for us to discuss." Now he was being evasive.

"Not tonight. Tonight is for us," Jack whispered seductively in her ear.

"Are you avoiding something?" She sipped her

wine with a frown. The kids avoided topics when they were holding out on something. Was she being paranoid again, or was Jack keeping something from her?

They showered together, but he dressed in the room while Kimberly put herself together in the bathroom. When she came out, dressed in a long, flowing aqua dress with a slit up the side, she nearly snatched Jack's breath away. Her feathery hair had lightened from the sun, giving it more of a streaked appearance. And while the dress didn't hug her like a second skin, there was enough cling so that her generous curves were displayed to perfection.

"Baby, I'm going to need my boxing gloves. You look so fabulous, I'm going to have to fight the guys off."

"Jack Canter. If I wasn't already married to you, I'd ask you to marry me," Kimberly said.

He laughed and kissed her. "Well, it's a good thing you already have me, or I'd have to say 'yes.'"

The smile she gave him was warm, and tears gathered in her eyes. He wiped them away with his thumb. "I love you, Kim. You know that."

She only nodded, so he kissed her again. He went in for a light peck, but she smelled so damn good that he gathered her close and deepened the kiss.

"If we don't stop, we won't make it to dinner," he said a few minutes later. "And I won't be able to show off my beautiful wife."

He never understood why Kimberly was so unsure about their marriage. They'd been together for seventeen years. Where did she think he was going? She rarely mentioned it, but he could read her expressions and moods. The skyrocketing divorce rate had no bearing on his feelings for her and their lives together.

Yes, the kids took up a lot of time. But soon it would be just the two of them. He didn't want their affection to be so far gone that they'd have to fight their way back together. To find out who they were as a couple all over again. He realized their interests were changing, and he didn't like that. He, too, felt torn. But he was still here. His goal was to find a way to work through her insecurities. They had time on their side. They were still young. Once all their futures were insured, he could slow down.

And he knew where Kimberly's insecurities came from. Her mother always told Kimberly she had to look out for herself. Nona's husband may have left her, but that did not mean Jack planned to leave Kimberly.

If Kimberly would be reasonable and cut her hours, they'd have more time together.

Jack knew Kimberly's mother was the reason she kept her job at the station. *Always have a source of income. Don't depend on a man or you could end up starting a new career in your fifties, making barely above minimum wage and competing with twenty-somethings. How could you ever catch up?* And Kimberly worked herself to death, between her job and the children.

He made enough to take care of his family. He worked the hours of two people, keeping those brew-pubs going. Her mother visited them a month ago and started yakking to Kimberly, this time about Lauren. *Keep an eye on that woman, or she'll walk off with your husband. That's how it happened with mine.*

But Jack knew that Nona's nagging probably drove her ex–old man crazy. He had no choice but to run off—to get some peace. Jack certainly hoped Kimberly didn't turn into a shrew.

Every year, he pretended he was too busy to take the trip home with her to Chicago, where her mother lived. And every year Kimberly nagged him for weeks about it, but he knew her well enough to know Lauren's presence was a thorn in her side. They'd talk about that.

There was nothing he could do to assure her that, no matter what problems they had, he wouldn't cheat on her. It was something she had to believe for herself.

Jack perused his wife as they headed out the door. She looked beautiful, with those expressive brown eyes. He kissed her on the tip of her nose and offered his arm. "Are you ready, madam?"

Jack peered closely at her abdomen. Was she pregnant? Was she holding that information back?

She placed her hand through his arm and they left the room.

Chapter 3

"Remember our honeymoon?" Jack asked, as they strolled toward the hotel proper. There were three restaurants at the resort, but they would dine at Hoby's, Jack and Kimberly's favorite.

"I remember."

They'd taken a trip to the Caribbean. Jack had borrowed a friend's sailboat. He was new at sailing, and when a sudden storm came up they'd ended up on Canter Island. Only, it wasn't named Canter at the time. Back then, it was privately owned, its lone inhabitant an old recluse.

"When the man exploded out of the woods with that double-barreled shotgun pointed at us, I thought we were dead for sure."

Kimberly shuddered. "Me, too." The wily man's face had resembled crinkled leather. It was a scary experience, facing a weapon and not knowing if that moment was your last. Kimberly couldn't help the quiver that jolted her again. Goose bumps covered her arms.

"I was afraid for you." Jack tightened an arm around her shoulder, drawing her closer. Kimberly soaked up the warmth of his body. "You were pregnant with my baby. We hadn't even been married three days, and this crazy old man was about to take us out."

Kimberly caught the hint of pride in Jack's voice when he mentioned the baby. Had he been proud? Had he been happy?

"He didn't tolerate anybody invading his space." Kimberly had been frightened out of her mind. "You shoved me behind your back. My hero." She reached up and caressed his jaw.

Jack's lips quirked. "Didn't quite work, because you came out fussing and threatening, waving your fist at the guy—and *he* held the gun." Jack shook his head because he'd lived through years of Kimberly's temper, but that particular incident topped them all. "I couldn't believe you."

"It worked, didn't it? Barnabas put the gun away."

"I guess so. With the way we were fighting with each other, his objections got lost in the cross fire."

"Barnabas Hoby turned out to be a nice old man," Kimberly said, smiling at the memory.

"I wouldn't call him 'nice,'" Jack hazarded, stopping to gaze up at the full moon before focusing on his wife.

"You were the only one he was nice to. Of course, he told me once that my punishment was being married to you."

Kimberly hit his arm.

"Ouch. Those were his words, not mine, baby," he said, laughing and dancing back a couple of steps, as Kimberly chased him.

"I'm not convinced." But it *was* something Barnabas would say, with his droll sense of humor. She imagined he hadn't cracked a smile. Sometimes it took a moment or two to even realize he'd told a joke.

"At least he let us sleep in his old hut." Kimberly had such warm memories of their honeymoon. Barnabas even managed to unearth a set of clean sheets. He'd shared his dinner and told them about his family around a campfire, after the storm passed over. He'd won the island in a card game and had lived there ever since.

Kimberly never understood why someone would want to live away from society, with no medical facilities at hand or other people to talk to. But he assured them he was never lonely. He had his parrot, dogs and cats.

The next day, he gave them directions back to the island where their hotel was located.

They visited Barnabas every two years, until he died six years ago. On one of their visits, he asked Jack what he would do if he owned the island. Jack had been truthful about his desire to build a resort. The lush vegetation was still there. Some of it was thick woodland, with knobby cypress trees whipped by tropical storms.

After he died, Jack and Kimberly collaborated with

Jack's brothers and sisters to buy the island and construct the resort.

Jack felt a measure of triumph and satisfaction. "From that first night we stayed here, I wanted this place, but I never knew how we could end up with it. Barnabas wasn't about to lose this place in another card game, and he wouldn't dream of selling it. We didn't have a spare nickel, so even if he was willing to sell it we couldn't afford to buy it."

"This was his home. You never told me how you could afford the honeymoon." Kimberly's voice was low and soft.

"My father taught me to save part of every dollar I made. I nearly cleaned out my bank account because I wanted you to have that special occasion to remember for the rest of our lives. Something to tell our children and grandchildren." An experience that was made even more significant thanks to Barnabas.

Kimberly stumbled to a halt and turned into Jack's arms, which closed loosely around her. Regardless of how furious he made her, he had a knack of making sweet gestures that made her heart turn over. "Oh, Jack." Tears came to her eyes. "I'll never forget it."

Jack scoffed. "It was a disaster."

"A disaster?" she said, astounded and puzzled. "It was wonderful. Even getting shipwrecked. I loved every moment of our honeymoon. Oh, Jack, we had such fun. Every day was filled with a million things to do, and we did them together. How could you possibly think it was a disaster?"

Her face was animated, full of joy and delight. Jack

kissed the tip of her nose before they started walking again. "It was fun, wasn't it? But we kept getting into scrapes. You almost drowned trying to scuba dive."

"We learned by trial and error."

In the old days, Kimberly went along with Jack's plans. She thought he was crazy for wanting to build the resort, but he'd shown her designs of what he wanted. Jack could always look at a situation and see the opportunities and possibilities.

He'd talk about his plans until Kimberly could envision his dreams as clearly as if they were her own. She wasn't hard to convince.

In the old days. But all that had changed—and Jack couldn't remember when the changes started to occur.

He wanted the old Kimberly back, that sweet young woman who dreamed with him. The one who looked up at him with respect and admiration.

"There's a beach party tonight," Kimberly said. "We better get dinner so we won't miss it."

"I want jerk chicken," Jack said. "Reminiscing has brought back the meal Barnabas prepared for us." Barnabas had taught Kimberly how to prepare the chicken, and now "Hoby's Jerk Chicken" was a part of the hotel's menu and one of the most popular items.

Jack ran a hand down Kimberly's arm and pulled her close. Was she pregnant? If so, why didn't she tell him? Did she think he'd be displeased? The news would make him the happiest man in the world.

Devin Canter sat at the table with his brother Jack and wiped the sweat from his brow. They were at the beach, where a band had started up. And since Jack gazed on like a spectator, Devin had danced the past three songs with Kimberly. The woman had boundless energy and wasn't ready to stop. She stayed on the dance floor while Devin returned to the table.

"I can't keep up with your wife. But I think *you* might need a couple more naps to keep up."

"I know how to deal with my wife," Jack said, knowing very well he was telling a lie. He didn't know how to deal with her any longer.

"Well, you need to start doing something. Enjoy your dinner?"

Jack sipped his rum. "Excellent. This place has improved every year since you took over."

Devin nodded. "You want to tell me why your wife was hanging on the beach by her lonesome today? Man, I had to fight off the guys. Christ. What's got into you? Leave a fine-looking woman like that on her own on your honeymoon?"

"Don't start getting on my case. I'm still older than you. And I can still whup your tail," he joked. "Kimberly isn't looking for another man. I don't have that to worry about."

"You forget your steps are slower these days. Didn't Kim say something about you needing a midday nap?"

"Keep it up. You're going to be missing some of those thirty-twos."

"The day I can't whup an old man is the day I hang up my boxing gloves."

They watched Kimberly do the limbo. Jack had seen her drinking a few rum punches earlier, so he realized she probably wasn't pregnant. Damn. Leaning low to go under the bar. Her head thrown back, she was smiling. Jack enjoyed seeing her happy. He frowned. He wasn't the only one watching her. Leaning back the way she was revealed the top of her cleavage. He frowned at some old man checking her out.

"I thought I'd need to bring out my kickboxing on that one," Devin said, nodding toward the very same man who'd accosted Kimberly earlier. "Had a hard time understanding the meaning of 'no.'"

A woman who appeared to be in her midfifties was sitting near the man, talking to other women at their table. When he was alone he'd have a few words with the man about hassling his wife. Why hadn't Kimberly said anything when she returned to the room?

His gaze skittered to Kimberly again. Barefoot, her painted toenails stood out in stark relief, and a gold ankle bracelet sparkled in the light. She moved gracefully beneath the bar, the split in her skirt showing an ample amount of leg, but she was still decent—though just barely. Jack had a good mind to go get her, but she'd bite his head off.

"You've got it made, man. A woman who loves you for you. You didn't have two nickels to rub together when you married, yet it didn't matter to her."

"I know."

"Hard to find a woman you can trust today. My ex couldn't wait to quit her job after the wedding. A wedding I paid for, by the way."

Jack tore his gaze from Kimberly, peering at his brother's sad face, and he wished for him the happiness he'd enjoyed with Kimberly and the children. "The right one will come along. You just have to stop being the player and turn back into the nice guy you are. A good woman wants to know she can trust you."

Shaking his head, Devin sneered the words of an embittered man. "Look where being good got me."

"You can't distrust all women because of what one did. They aren't all like Keisha."

"You've been married too long to know today's lay of the land. They're just looking for a sugar daddy, and make no bones about it." The bitterness in his tone worried Jack.

"That woman has your mind twisted. All women aren't like her. No sense in me saying it, because you won't listen, but I'm going to say it anyway. There's someone out there who's going to knock you off your feet one day, and she's going to make you work for her affection, but she isn't going to trust a playa." Jack couldn't believe he was lecturing his brother like a busybody old woman. But his brother needed a brush with reality.

"Right," Devin mocked. "I'm holding my breath for that day."

"You should be." Jack stretched out his long legs. "I just wish Kim would quit her job and come home. I tell you, she's becoming one stubborn woman. Sometimes it's like talking to a brick wall."

"If the fact that she's working is your biggest complaint, you've got nothing to complain about. Women like a little independence these days."

"Mama never complained about being home."

"Kim isn't Mom. And I hope you have sense enough not to mention that."

"Of course I do, but I hate to see her work herself half to death. Look at her. She's rested here, not tired and grumpy like she is when she's overworked and running herself ragged. Then she runs after the kids. Not to mention the PTA. She has a one-on-one relationship with all the children's teachers. She's on every committee in every activity the children are involved in, and then there's other volunteer work associated with the TV station. The woman doesn't have time to breathe."

"You can help her with the children and the PTA." Devin glanced at Kimberly again. "I repeat, you've got it good, man. You have your businesses. It makes you feel good about yourself, that you can provide well for your family. Kim needs something more, too. Or are you one of those knuckleheads who think you know what's best for her, or that her life should revolve only around you?"

Jack sent his brother an impatient glance. "We do have children, you know."

"Teenagers, not babies."

Jack scowled at his wife. Kimberly bent so low that, with a high-pitched squeal, she fell flat on the ground and started laughing again.

"Damn it…" Jack rose to his feet, rushing over to help her up. He stared at the four guys who also rushed forward to assist her.

"Excuse me." His angry gaze had them backing up. He scooped her up. She was still laughing as she lay languid in his arms.

Jack shook his head. With her infectious spirit, Kimberly wrapped everyone around her pinky. That was when she wasn't rushing to work every day, then rushing home to deal with the kids' after-school activities and homework. She took more time with her appearance. He didn't have to watch her on the TV to see her looking good.

Jack sighed. She refused to understand that she wasn't the same happy person when she was overworked.

But she was his.

"I've had enough," Kimberly said, laughing. She didn't know the last time she'd had so much fun. She dusted off her dress. "I must look a mess," she said, sitting at the table beside Devin to take a breather.

"My brother can't take his eyes off you," Devin said.

"Be serious." She knew that was a lie, but she couldn't help the blush heating up her cheeks.

"I'm serious."

Kimberly's stomach fluttered at the thought. Jack was so very handsome tonight, in an island shirt with tan linen slacks. Standing with one hand dug deep into his pockets as he talked to the island's physician, he seemed the epitome of a *GQ* man.

The sand felt wonderful beneath her feet and between her toes. She loved coming to this place. It was as if the weight of the world had lifted from her shoulders.

"Are you ready to call it a night?" Jack asked Kimberly, just as the performer belted into a slow, soulful song.

"Not quite. You haven't danced with me."

He pulled her up and strolled over the sand to where other couples were dancing. The singer was belting oldies. Many of the women were just watching and grooving with the music, their feet and arms moving to the beat. There were always more women than men. That was something Kimberly had noticed lately, wherever she went. But these women exuded energy. They knew how to have fun with or without men. That was what she liked about the island.

Closing his arms around her, Jack pulled her close. Heat radiating from his body warmed her as they moved to the rhythm. It was a change of pace from the energetic dances of before. She rubbed her hand up his chest around to his back. He groaned in her ear, his sweet breath brushing against her lobe.

"You're going to end up in trouble right here on the sand," Jack rumbled.

Desire rushed up Kimberly's spine. "Too many people."

"Don't count on it," he said, nuzzling her neck and pulling her closer. He maneuvered them so they were apart from the others and her back was to the crowd.

Kimberly was feeling no pain. "It's not often I get your undivided attention. I'm taking advantage of it," she said, listening to the rhythmic rush of the waves mixing with the band. She slid her hand under Jack's shirt.

"You've got to stop that, baby."

A smile touched her face. "Are you sure?"

"I'm sure it's time for us to go to our room."

"Hmm. I want to tease you a little more."

"You're tipsy."

"I am not," she scoffed, then hiccupped.

Jack chuckled, stroking her with a loving touch. "You never could drink."

"I don't have to worry about it tonight," Kimberly said as she kissed him. "I'm not driving."

"Woman, you're going to end up with more than you bargained for."

"Is that a promise?" she asked hopefully.

Jack wrapped his arm around her shoulder and she wrapped hers around his waist, as they strolled away from the beach and toward their cabana.

The resort wasn't too large or too formal, but it was an upscale, casual, laid-back, comfortable setting. With three hundred rooms, several cabanas and a couple of villas, it was booked year-round, and reservations had to be made months in advance. It wasn't a huge island, but it was self-contained and had ample room, so that the guests didn't feel crowded. There were boats at the harbor ready to escort them to other islands—places that offered other amenities, like gambling. Snorkeling, parasailing and deep-sea fishing were very popular here.

Tonight, however, Jack's mind was on his wife.

"You look well rested," he said.

"So do you. You work too hard, Jack." She rubbed his chest.

"I guess we both do. That's why I want you to quit your job. You look so much happier now."

"Of course I'm happy. I'm with you."

"You look tired most of the time at home."

"Jack, you're always tired, too, but I'm not asking you to quit your job."

"A man has to work, Kim. He's got to provide for his family."

She was butting against his sense of responsibility. "You provide more than we can ever use. And I appreciate it, really I do, but I'd like to spend more time with you." She glanced at him. "I don't want to lose you in the meantime."

"That's not going to happen."

Kimberly nodded, but Jack knew she didn't believe him.

"I'm considering job-sharing again," she said.

"You don't have to work at all. And you can take some time off while you wait for the right position, if you feel you must."

"But I've been at that station for more than ten years. I have benefits—retirement, insurance. If anything ever happened…"

"Nothing will," he said quickly, as the shadow of his father passed through his mind. "Lots of women would love the opportunity to spend more time at home. You know we don't need the money. And you could come to the island anytime you wanted to."

"Alone," Kimberly said. "Your schedule won't let you come with me. Honey, I don't want to talk about work now."

Jack sighed. "You're a stubborn woman, Kimberly Canter. Sometimes too stubborn."

Kimberly sighed, too. "You don't have any room to talk there."

They neared the courtyard of their cabana. Jack pulled her close and kissed her. She'd fired his blood so hot that he wanted to take her to bed and make love to her for the rest of the night.

"We have to take this inside," he said, fumbling the key in the door and shoving it open, pulling her in behind him. They barely made it to the bed before she tumbled onto it and he went down after her.

"You've been teasing me all night," he gasped, as he shoved her dress up and kissed her thigh. "No wonder that man couldn't keep his eyes off you. You captivated me the first time I laid eyes on you."

"Is that right?"

"You know it is," he said, nipping her lightly—and when she moaned, he soothed the injury with his tongue.

She dug her fingers into his shoulders, then caressed the strong muscles bunching beneath her fingertips. He was hard and smooth at once.

He moved up her body and kissed her, settling his weight on her and driving his tongue deep into the cavern of her mouth. Their tongues dueled a mating dance, igniting a fire so hot only his soothing touch could calm the flames.

He rolled her over so that she was on top, and slowly unzipped her dress, caressing the smooth, soft skin beneath. Her fingers were busy unbuttoning his shirt, then she ran them through the hair on his chest, bent and suckled on his nipple.

He groaned and inched the dress up her thighs, cupping her butt in his hand and squeezing the cheeks lightly.

She eased his zipper down and captured the thickness of him in her hand, massaging him back and forth.

He groaned deep in his throat. "I can't take much more of this, baby."

"You won't have to," Kimberly said. She eased up and Jack peeled her thong down her legs, his eyes widening as he realized what little scraps of fabric had covered her as she'd danced on the beach.

"I need to lock you up and throw away the key."

"Welcome to the twenty-first century, baby."

"Your skirt tail was hiked up most of the night."

Affronted, Kimberly pinched his chest then kissed it well. "It was not. Everything was discreetly covered."

"I know I saw a lot of thigh when you were doing the limbo."

"That's all you could see from the split."

Jack groaned. "I noticed."

"Remember that the next time you leave me on my own," she said, her voice hitching when Jack stroked her intimately. A tremble inside heated her thighs and groin. He knew just where and how to touch her until passion rose in her like a searing flame.

Jack moaned again as she leaned up, then seated herself, easing down on him slowly, breath easing from her in a rush. His gaze impaling her, he clutched her hips and moved his until she was stretched fully with him. Moving deeply within her, he stoked a fire so hot that her breath hissed with sheer joy. And the burning flames she saw in his eyes drove her wild. His tormented groans were heady music to her ears.

He stretched her thighs wider, until she felt him deep inside. "Oh, Jack," she cried out, her voice strangled.

"You want me as much as I want you." It was a command. He pulled out of her until she could feel only the very tip of him.

"Yes! Yes," she cried, wanting—desperately needing—every inch of him inside her.

When he filled her again, Kimberly sighed with pleasure. She moved her hips and their bodies slapped against each other, building the passion, until that moment—that precious moment—when electricity seemed to arc through her and she heard his deep bellow of fulfillment ringing in the air, overshadowing her own cries of pleasure.

The turbulence of fulfillment swirled around them. She crashed on his chest, feeling the staccato beat of his heart. He stroked her back until they had breath enough to move. Then shifting slightly, he spooned her against him.

Kimberly had such a lovely evening, it was the next morning before she remembered Jack's work. They dined on their patio, surrounded by hibiscus flowers, and watched the waves.

Jack seemed to be brooding.

"What is it?" After last night, Kimberly didn't think anything could crush her good mood.

"Are you pregnant?"

Kimberly coughed. "Are you kidding?"

"No." Jack chewed a piece of mango. "I know I saw

you drinking last night, but I can't help but wonder…
I mean, you aren't using protection." He paused with
another piece of fruit inches from his mouth. "Are
you?"

"No. I haven't used protection in years. But, Jack,
we've tried and tried to have another baby and
couldn't. I'm not pregnant."

His chest expanded on a huge breath of air. "I see."

"Think about it. The kids are nearly grown. Do you
really want a child at your age? Do you really want to
start all over again with diapers? It was okay when we
first tried. Byron was only five and April was three.
There wasn't that great an age difference between
them."

"I guess not," Jack said, but Kimberly could tell he
was displeased, and some of the joy of the previous
night seemed to dissipate.

Kimberly ate a slice of melon. She hadn't thought
of having babies in years. She reached over and
gently touched his hand. "I'm ready for us to have
some time together, Jack. Before you know it, we'll
have grandbabies."

"God, not too soon, I hope. April's way too young
to be even thinking of boys. And Byron's got an entire
future in front of him."

"They are at that age. You had better be prepared for
it."

"Well, I'm not." With his mouth creased in a stubborn line, he attacked his food again.

Kimberly shook her head and smothered a smile.

"I signed us up for a massage this morning," she

said, pleased at the image of them lying on adjacent massage tables.

"I can't go," Jack said, not meeting her gaze. "I'm going to finish some work I have to e-mail out later today."

"It's couple massages. Let's forget about the work for a couple of days. You promised."

"I know, but I got a call, and I have to finish something by this afternoon." He smiled softly. "By the time you get out of your massage, I'll be finished, and we'll have the rest of the day and tomorrow together."

"We're going home in a couple of days," Kimberly said. "We wasted yesterday."

He sent her one of those looks designed to get the heat stirring. "I seem to remember some great moments."

"But, Jack, I have more planned than making love," Kimberly insisted. "Although I enjoyed it very much."

He nodded in satisfaction. "I'm sorry, baby. I can't get a massage," he said firmly.

"What are you working on that's so important it has to interfere with our honeymoon?"

He sighed, swallowed some orange juice. "I'm running through the numbers and feasibility of opening another brewpub."

Kimberly's eyes widened. After a moment she said, "Without even discussing it with me? We never see you as it is. If you open another one, I'll really never see you. You know how hands-on you are."

"The timing is good, and it's a deal that's too good

to turn down. I want this place, Kim. I was going to run the numbers and studies before I discussed it with you."

"They're all too good to turn down. I know you, Jack. I never complained about your working long hours in the past, but I'm complaining now. What about our lives?" Kimberly entreated. "We have no time together now. Even on vacation work intrudes. Opening a new brewpub takes months. You missed April's birth because of them."

"Are you going to bring this up every time we have a fight? That's why I hired Lauren, so she can take up some of the slack."

"She doesn't take up the slack. You're working as hard as ever, even though she's there," Kimberly said, scooting back in her chair. "Lauren's in love with you."

"Don't be ridiculous, Kim. She's an employee. I don't fraternize with employees. You know that."

"You refuse to see it, don't you? Is it because you have feelings for her, too?"

Anger darkening his eyes, Jack leaned in close to her. "I have always been faithful to you, Kim. I'm not even going to entertain this line of thought. It's ridiculous." With an angry swing of his wrist, he tossed his napkin on the table.

"Our family can't stand one more brewpub, Jack."

Jack threw up his hands. "I'm just running through the numbers. That's all."

"During the time you should be spending with me. You said this would be our time together. I spent yesterday alone."

"I'm a businessman. I either grow or die."

"The children rarely see you. They'll be out of the house soon," Kimberly shot back.

"I have breakfast with them every morning."

"But lately you miss all their games. You used to never miss them. They see you for how long? Fifteen minutes, while they shovel food in their mouths on their way out the door?"

"I've dedicated my life to you and those children."

Pain radiated from the depths of her eyes. "There's a difference between financial support and emotional support."

"You want me to do all the bending. I've asked you to quit a job that you don't even need. Then you'll have all your time for the children. You don't need to work at all."

"I get off at noon. I'm home when they get there. I have weekends off. Working part-time wouldn't change anything. Except that I'll be more lonely than ever, because you still wouldn't have any more time to spend with me. Besides, I like having cleaning people come in every week. I kept the house clean before I started working, but it isn't my favorite job."

"We can afford the cleaning staff. I don't expect you to clean that huge house. We can afford a live-in. Money isn't an issue."

Kimberly rubbed her forehead. She felt a headache coming on.

"I promised you I'd take care of you when I married you, and I do that," Jack said.

"I'm not talking about money. I want a partner.

Jack, we've grown apart. We don't do anything together anymore. We live in the same house, but live separate lives. I don't want that kind of relationship."

He glanced at his watch, wiped his mouth with his napkin. "This is a fruitless argument. There's no reasoning with you. I have a few calls to make, and if you don't get to the spa you're going to miss your massage."

Kimberly clenched her hands together. "This is important, Jack. We need to discuss this. Whenever we broach this topic you run off."

"You're making a mountain out of a molehill, baby. By the time you finish up, we can do something together. We'll make plans when you get back."

Kimberly clenched her teeth together to keep her voice from trembling. "I signed us up for snorkeling this afternoon."

"Great. I'll be ready," he said. "I'll meet you in the restaurant for an early lunch at eleven. That way, we can relax a bit before we get in the water." He kissed her lightly on the lips and started back to the room.

"But, Jack…"

"Eleven sharp." He waved to her and kept walking.

Losing yet another battle, Kimberly headed to the spa. She was miserable, at her wits' end, trying to figure a way to reach Jack. She knew that if they didn't find some middle ground, the marriage wouldn't last. She'd seen the way her parents had grown apart over the years. The same thing was happening to her and she couldn't do a thing to stop it—not alone. It was like a train wreck waiting to happen.

Kimberly sighed. Maybe the massage would relax her. This vacation certainly wasn't. She should have brought the children. At least she'd have someone to explore the island with—and they'd enjoy the trip. It wasn't that she was incapable or afraid to be on her own. She spent most of her time alone or with friends. But the game plan was, the weekend should be like a second honeymoon—and this was as far from their first honeymoon as they could possibly get.

Jack hung up the phone and glanced at his watch. Damn it. It was eleven-thirty. He was late meeting Kimberly. She was going to kill him anyway, as soon as he told her they had to leave a day early. But he had no choice. The area was changing. A large company just bought property nearby to build an office building. Another was building a condo on the next block. Lauren could do part of the draft, but he needed to finalize everything before the Tuesday meeting. He needed to work all day Sunday. But at least they had a couple of days together, which was better than nothing.

Grabbing his wallet, he strolled briskly out of the room, heading to the restaurant. Hopefully, Kimberly was still there. She was a slow eater, so more than likely she would be.

But when Jack arrived, Kimberly was nowhere to be seen. He didn't see her on the way, so where the heck could she be? They only had the afternoon left. He'd had his secretary reserve early morning flights. Why wasn't Kim where she was supposed to be? He reached for his cell phone to call her, but realized he'd left it in the room.

* * *

When Kimberly reached the room, Jack was no-where to be found. But his cell phone was on the desk along with business papers. She had to change quickly if she wanted to make their snorkeling appointment. Obviously, he wasn't interested. She'd stop by the dining room on her way out, just in case he was late.

But she wasn't going to miss her snorkeling. She should get something out of this ill-fated weekend.

Kimberly quickly changed, grabbed the things she needed and made a quick trip by the restaurant—where she didn't see Jack.

"Going snorkeling?"

Kimberly turned abruptly, thinking Jack was behind her, but it was Devin. "Jack and I were supposed to go together, but he's MIA. No surprise there."

"Where is he?"

"I haven't a clue. I have to go or I'll be late."

"You need a partner."

"Maybe another person in the group will need a partner, too."

"Hold up a minute. I'm going with you. I'll meet you at the pier in ten minutes."

Kimberly was on the boat before her cell phone rang. She had a good mind to ignore it, but she an-swered.

"Where are you?" Jack asked.

"Where do you think I am? I'm on the boat."

"Why didn't you come by to get me?"

Kimberly was too full of anger for words. *He was the one who didn't show up and he asks me?* "I must have sat at the wrong table at lunch, because obviously I didn't see you."

"The time got away from me. You should have called."

"We're almost out of range," she said and hung up. She wanted to toss the phone in the ocean. But she turned it off and stuck it into her bag.

Her eyes veered to the horizon. Devin patted her hand. "He loves you. Just remember that."

Kimberly was too angry to respond.

"Beautiful day, isn't it?" someone beside her said.

Kimberly used her television face to control her erratic emotions and nodded. She even managed to produce a smile. "Yes, it is."

"My daughter and I take a trip once a year before the high tourist season. I just love it. Usually, we come in the winter after hurricane season, but both of us had projects that prevented us this time. Those currents can get vicious after a storm."

"I usually come every summer," Kimberly said.

"I'm Shelly, and this is my daughter, Casey. I was just telling her that you look familiar."

"Where are you from?" Kimberly asked.

"D.C."

"I'm a meteorologist," she said, naming the station she aired on. "I do the morning forecast."

"I knew I'd seen you before. But I thought your hair was longer."

"I just cut it."

"That's why you look so different. I usually listen to you as I dress in the mornings."

Kimberly smiled.

The boat stopped and the guide anchored it. Then they were in the ocean—and the shock of the cold water gripped her breath until her body acclimated to the drop in temperature. It was truly a different world beneath the Caribbean water.

Many in the group were couples, and even though Devin was with her, Kimberly felt the loss intense and sharp. The tango of lovers. Legs touched. Warm looks. The dance of lovers beneath the waters she'd experienced with Jack on their first honeymoon. All that was missing.

The reefs were gorgeous. But it couldn't take the place of having her husband's undivided attention for a change. Was she asking for too much? Was she acting needy?

Kimberly had known the truth all along, but had managed to push it to the back of her mind. Jack didn't marry her because he wanted to, but because he felt obligated to. She finished college, but she'd always wondered, if she had not been pregnant, would he have married her at all? And was that the reason she couldn't keep his attention now? He felt an obligation to her and the children.

Kimberly felt tears welling up. But she couldn't afford to cry while wearing a mask. She forced them back. She loved Jack with every beat of her heart. But love meant having the strength to give him up if the relationship was stifling him.

More and more, she felt she was holding him in a place where he didn't want to be.

Chapter 4

*D*amn. *Kimberly will be really steamed when she returns,* Jack thought, deeply regretting his lateness. He couldn't help feeling annoyed, too. He shouldn't have to tiptoe around his wife to expand his business.

Since Kimberly was gone and there was no sense worrying, he might as well work. But the warm sun and the gentle breeze of the Caribbean beckoned him. He gathered his papers into his briefcase and trucked out to the beach, moving his lounge chair away from the others before he parked himself on it, with his cell phone close by. He was waiting for a call from Lauren. He might as well get the work finished. He and Kimberly were leaving in the morning.

He'd promised himself and Kimberly he'd never

give her a reason to regret marrying him, but he wondered sometimes if she did—if she sometimes wished she'd married that guy back home, from the wealthy family, safely established in a third-generation business. With him, she'd never have to worry about a catastrophe that could pull the rug from under your feet.

At least he'd chosen his locations well. Each of his brewpubs was making a profit.

And at least he and Kimberly had tonight together. Right now she wouldn't understand, but eventually, Jack was certain, she'd come around. Or would she? She was testy lately. In the past she always fell in line with his dreams. She understood the work required in owning your own business. But after all these years she was becoming more demanding.

The tropical breeze blew over his skin, relieving the heat a bit. He ordered a gin and tonic, then tried to reach Kimberly again. Her phone was turned off. The waiter served his drink, and after signing the check, he took a sip and opened his briefcase.

At least Kimberly was getting a vacation out of this. She was overworked. It was easy for her to think expanding wasn't important and that they had enough. There had been a time before his father died that his family had lived well. Beautiful house in D.C., in a nice safe neighborhood, nice clothes and cars. Everything a growing family needed. And at first, after his father's death, although stricken with grief, they managed to do well for a couple of years.

Then his mother remarried—a loser named Raymond. Raymond knew just how to win them all over.

He was one of those smooth-talking men who knew just the right words to say for every situation.

Jack wasn't that smooth-talking. He was more like his dad. He did what needed to be done to keep his family safe. But not his stepdad. Raymond managed to run through every cent Jack's late dad had amassed.

Jack and his older brothers were forced to work while they went to school, to help their mother make ends meet until she was able to function on her own.

His younger sisters and brothers wanted to work, too, but his mother assigned chores around the house for them to do.

Yes, Kimberly felt nice and safe in their huge house with four floors including the basement. The third floor alone was large enough to hold a family with three kids.

His dad had done well, too. Not quite as well as Jack had, but they had been comfortable. But what had taken his dad a lifetime to build, his stepfather had squandered in little over a year.

Life had a way of turning on a dime. Kimberly thought that because he wasn't around every moment the kids were home that he didn't spend enough time with them. What parent did, unless they were obsessive like her? Did he complain about that? He thought about the baby that was not to be and felt an abiding sense of loss.

It was late that afternoon before Kimberly made it back to the island. "Thanks for diving with me, Devin. I hope it wasn't too much of an imposition."

"Will you stop worrying? I enjoyed myself, sis. I'm at your service anytime." Squeezing her hand lightly, he left her at the door and drove away. A moment later, Kimberly let herself into the room.

It was a beautiful day after all, especially after she met the mother and daughter from D.C. And Devin certainly kept her entertained, relating childhood episodes with his brothers and sisters. She'd thought she'd heard them all, but Devin always revealed something new. She'd wished again that she could have brought the children along.

Will wonders ever cease, she thought, with a sarcastic look on her face. Jack was in the room, already dressed for dinner. He was opening a bottle of wine.

"Enjoy your snorkeling?" he had the nerve to ask.

"Yes," she replied without elaborating.

"I'm sorry you had to go alone."

Kimberly peeled off her clothes. "I'm accustomed to being alone."

Trying to keep a grip on his temper, Jack poured a glass of wine and handed it to her.

"Thank you."

"I picked out a nice little restaurant a short walk from here. I think you'll like it."

"I'll shower and get ready then." Kimberly was determined to avoid the subject of his absence. Just like she'd avoided it her entire marriage. She took the wineglass with her into the shower. The water felt good running over her body.

After she finished and toweled dry, she rubbed lotion all over, dried her hair and fixed it, and dressed carefully. At this point she didn't know what to do about her marriage. Perhaps it was because she'd let things go so long that Jack still had tunnel vision about their relationship. It was hard to be optimistic, but she tried to look on the bright side. At least they had two more days to talk, to work out their differences, before they returned home.

When she came out of the bathroom Jack gave her a long whistle. "You're gorgeous."

"Thank you," she said demurely.

He gave her a rose and they left for dinner. She hoped he didn't think that small gesture made up for his absence. She lifted the rose to her nose and inhaled. She tried not to put a negative spin on his actions. After all, the rose was a sweet gesture.

It was another lovely evening, with the energetic beat of calypso music. The brisk breeze blowing across the water had increased. They walked along the shore after they ate, she carrying her shoes in her hands.

"This is nice, isn't it?"

"Very. I wish we could stay longer," Jack said.

"We have a couple more days."

"I'm sorry, honey, but we have to leave tomorrow. I have a million things to go over for a Tuesday meeting."

Kimberly had promised herself she wouldn't argue, but Jack pushed all the wrong buttons. "If this wasn't a good time for you, why did we come?"

"The children were worried. I thought, if we got away together, it would ease some of their concerns."

"So this vacation wasn't about spending time together after all—or an attempt to build on our marriage."

"I'm sorry I couldn't spend more time with you, but…"

"If you had been up-front about this, then I could have made different plans," Kimberly said. "We didn't have to come here."

"Didn't you have a nice time?"

"But I thought I'd be spending the vacation with you, Jack. Aren't you even listening to me?"

"There was work to do."

"I work, too, but I take time out for our family. You have to take a more active role in the kids' lives. And I want a husband, not a bank."

"Yeah, well, when you want to buy something and you don't have to worry about the cost, you spin a different tune. You don't have to worry about where the kids' college money is coming from, do you?"

"Of course those things are important, but I want them to remember being part of a warm, loving family, too."

"I love my kids."

"I know you do. You married me for them, didn't you?"

"Are we back to that again? What did you expect me to do, Kim, leave you?" He sighed tiredly. "Kim, we're always going over circular arguments. There's no end to them. Here we are, on a lovely Caribbean island. We could be enjoying the evening, but you're fighting about nothing."

"Do you even want this marriage, Jack?" Kimberly asked softly.

"If I didn't I wouldn't be here. Does that answer your question once and for all?"

Silence stretched between them.

"Sometimes I wonder if you know me at all," Kimberly finally said.

"Why do we have to go through the same drama all the time? Why can't we enjoy this last night on the island together?"

"Because you do things without even considering my wants or needs. Why didn't you at least discuss it with me first?"

"I didn't see you today."

"And whose fault is that?"

"It's life. There's no reason to pass blame. It's unproductive."

Kimberly started walking toward the hotel. She wasn't a defeatist, but she finally admitted to herself she didn't know what to do to bring her husband around. If Jack didn't want to spend time with her, there was nothing she could do about it. More than ever, Kimberly believed that Jack kept his promise when he married her. He never said he'd love her forever, but that she'd never go without the things she and the children needed. He'd always provided a roof. They'd never gone hungry. She made good money, too, even before she went full-time, but it was a drop in the bucket compared to what the pubs and the resort netted.

But she was hungry for a need that a full stomach and a roof could never provide.

"Where are you going?" Jack asked.

"I have to pack."

Sighing, he followed her.

"Wait a minute. I don't need to leave." Suddenly, Kimberly stopped and faced him. "I've spent most of the vacation alone anyway. Why don't you go back and I'll stay?" All the time she'd spent trying to get him to see reason was for nothing.

"Is that what you want?"

"Just answer one question. What material thing do we need that we don't already have? The kids have so many clothes that the tags are still on some of the ones I give to charity. They have way more than they need, except time with you. We all have more material things than we need."

"You don't appreciate a thing I do for my family, do you?"

"I appreciate it, Jack. I just think we have our priorities skewed." She turned and continued into the cabana.

Jack wanted to tell Kimberly that, regardless of what they had now, life could turn on a dime. She could have all the clothes in the world, but when disaster struck, all of it could disappear like a puff of smoke.

But she wouldn't understand that. As much as he'd tried to convince her that they needed a secure future, she would never understand.

Of course he wanted to spend more time with his children. Of course he wanted more time with her. But couldn't she appreciate that he was trying to make sure she'd never suffer as his mom had? His father had provided, but they'd lost everything except the house. His family would never know what going to bed hungry felt like.

That night, Kimberly and Jack slept on opposite

sides of the king-size bed. Jack, with his arm thrown over his eyes. He didn't even try to bridge the distance.

Stewing in her inability to forge a meaningful bond with Jack, Kimberly hugged the opposite edge.

All Kimberly's dreams of a husband who loved her, and of growing old together, went up in smoke. With the exception of sex, they had nothing in common. They'd grown apart. Eventually, they'd end up like her parents. A year after Kimberly left for college her father had asked her mother for a divorce, and soon after moved in with a much younger woman. He'd given the excuse that he and his wife had nothing in common any longer. They'd grown too far apart, a gorge too wide to even try to connect. And truthfully, he didn't even want to try.

If their relationship continued as it was, Kimberly could see herself in the same situation after April left home.

In the middle of the night Kimberly's cell phone rang. Thinking something horrible had happened, she was surprised when she heard her producer's voice.

"The storm's coming closer to you than first predicted," he said without preamble. "I know you don't have coverage there. If I get a film crew to you from a feeder station, can you cover it?"

"How close is this storm supposed to hit?"

"Far enough away that the island doesn't have to be evacuated, but close enough that you'd get some of the effects. It's shifted. The path has moved a couple of hundred miles closer."

Kimberly wasn't too happy about being so close to

a hurricane, but when her producer mentioned it was predicted to be little more than a tropical storm, her concern diminished.

"I wouldn't ask you to stay if I thought you'd be in any danger," he said, when Kimberly hesitated. "You do have storm shelters on the island, don't you?"

"Of course. I'll do it," she finally said and hung up.

"Who was that?" Jack asked groggily.

"My producer. The hurricane is coming closer than they first predicted and they want me to cover it."

Jack slapped the covers back and sat up on his side of the bed. "Is he crazy? You're not staying here to cover a hurricane."

"Don't worry," Kimberly assured him. "It's not going to hit this island."

Jack stood, rounding on her. "I'm not leaving you here with a hurricane looming. I hope you have sense enough not to argue about this."

"I'm staying," she said adamantly. "If I run into trouble, Devin is here."

"That's not the point. You're leaving on the plane with me in the morning."

"I'm staying." She turned her back to him and pulled the covers up to her shoulders.

"Kimberly, your stubbornness borders on insanity. You don't even need the damn job. Is it the reason you never got pregnant again?"

"What?" Kimberly slapped the covers back and pushed into a sitting position.

"We tried for years to have another child, but conveniently, we never did."

"How the heck did we get from the storm to us? You're the one who refused to have tests done. I took them."

"We had two children already," Jack scoffed, brushing aside the implications. "We already knew we could produce. Were you taking the pill on the side and didn't tell me about it?"

"Don't you even trust me?" Kimberly asked sadly, shocked that he'd even think she'd do something so underhanded. "I never took the pill. I still don't."

"All I know is I wanted another child. You were reluctant about it in the beginning because you didn't want another child to interfere with your job, the way it interfered with school."

"Even with two children, I still got my degree."

"But a job is different. Perhaps you didn't want another child to cut in on your work time."

"Why do you think I earned a college degree, if not to work?"

"Every woman with a degree doesn't necessarily work for a paying job. Many do volunteer work."

"I do volunteer work. And I didn't lie to you about trying to have a baby," Kimberly said emphatically. "I can't believe you're bringing this up. If we'd had another child, I'd have raised it alone, just like the other two."

"You weren't alone."

"You weren't in the delivery room with April. No doubt you would have been working through the third one, too."

"You know how badly I felt about that."

"Humph. Why should I? I wasn't the underhanded

one. I'm not the secretive one. I had tests done. And nothing was wrong with me."

"So you're saying it was me."

"I don't know. My gynecologist says it just happens that way sometimes."

The color drained from Jack's face. "You talked our personal business over with her?"

"Of course. She's my doctor."

"She's also your sorority sister."

"First and foremost, she's a doctor," Kimberly snapped. "She wouldn't discuss patients' personal lives with anyone. Do your frat brothers discuss patients' personal information with you? Besides, if you remember, Vicky wasn't my gynecologist at the time. She was still in medical school when we decided to have another child. So your secret is safe."

"There's nothing wrong with me."

"I didn't say there was," Kimberly said. "Why are we having this argument now? Do you really want another baby now? You're thirty-eight. I'm thirty-five. We aren't in our twenties anymore. And, Jack, I sat up late at night when the kids were teething or colicky. You never lost a night's sleep. Why wouldn't it be that way if we had another child? It's all good when you don't have to bother with all the problems and details."

There was a pause, then, "If I didn't participate, it's because you were always there to do it. And besides, I was working sixteen- to twenty-hour days then."

Kimberly turned away from Jack again and pulled the covers tight against her neck.

"Damn it! Woman, I'm talking to you."

"I'm not listening anymore. Now suddenly, I'm not trustworthy. We're discussing an issue that has no meaning any longer."

Jack stomped to the bathroom. Kimberly heard the toilet flush. When he came back, he dressed and left the room.

Slowly, Kimberly turned on her back. The moonlight filtered in and she stared at the ceiling, studying the shadows. She wondered if Jack was sitting outside stewing.

Even now, she could hear the wind increasing in intensity. If it kept going like this, the plane wouldn't be allowed to take off tomorrow and Jack would be stuck here with her, which was the last place he wanted to be right now. And truthfully, she wanted some distance from him, too.

Kimberly sighed. She wasn't quitting her job.

Although Jack was very generous, she didn't like the idea of every little trinket she purchased having to come from him.

If she were honest, her mother wasn't the only reason she worked. She enjoyed her job. And she didn't understand why Jack felt it was so important for her to quit. In addition to money, she needed to be emotionally satisfied, too.

But once Jack started with a situation, he'd gnaw on it the way a dog gnawed on a bone. There was absolutely no reasoning with him.

His wife was the most unreasonable woman he'd ever met, Jack thought several hours later, as he came back to his room with a cup of coffee. He'd finally fallen asleep in the lounger outside. When the sun rose he came inside and took a shower. Kimberly was sleeping without a care in the world. He went in search of another cup of coffee. The wind had already increased, and most of the hotel guests were leaving before the storm came in. People with sense, that is. A few diehards stuck it out, getting every last penny out of their resort package.

When he returned after breakfast, Kimberly had left.

Sitting in Devin's office, Kimberly sipped her coffee during a conference call with other weather forecasters at various stations on the East Coast. This was their usual MO when a hurricane hit. They consulted with each other, predicting the patterns according to data readouts.

Jack should be on the boat, navigating the choppy water to the main island to catch his flight. She tried to focus on the positive. They'd spent some time together, and when they were together—and not fighting—they enjoyed each other's company.

"Kim, how is the weather on Canter Island?" a coworker asked her.

"The wind's been increasing throughout the night. I expect the storm to hit in about three hours."

They talked for another fifteen minutes before everyone disconnected and rushed to write up their findings for their next news bite. Kimberly returned to the cabana.

"I thought you were going to catch the early flight

out," she said, surprised Jack was still there. She didn't know how she felt about his presence. In the heat of anger, he'd said he was going to stay, but she hadn't expected him to. Not with his all-important meeting looming.

"Do you really think I'd leave you here, with a hurricane on the way?"

Her brows shadowed her eyes. "Jack, I wanted you to go back to be with the children."

"My mother's with them. They're fine. I talked to her earlier."

"Well, the crew should be here soon."

He nodded. They both fell silent, as if they were strangers who'd lost their ability to communicate. She wore a rain slicker. Light rain had begun that morning, and now it was pouring heavily. Kimberly held her face up, gazing around.

"I'm going inside to get a couple of things before I leave. What are you going to do?"

"I'm going with you."

"I'm going to be filming."

As if she needed to remind him. "I know. You're not going out of my sight."

She tightened her lips. "I can do my job."

"We both know I can't stop you," he snapped.

"Don't start it now." She disappeared inside. By the time she returned, a ragged-looking Jeep pulled to a stop in front of their cabin.

Jack approached and spoke to the men. He got into, then started his brother's SUV. When Kimberly came out he called to her, "We're following them."

She nodded and climbed inside, then they drove to the opposite edge of the island.

"Did this thing shift again?" Jack asked.

"Feels like it. It's increasing in intensity, too. It was always windier on this side of the island."

The Jeep in front of them rocked when a huge gust of wind whipped by. "I'm grateful for this truck," Kimberly said. Although their SUV was heavier, it still had the potential of tipping over in the storm.

Jack grunted as he drove ahead, wondering how crazy his wife really was.

The water was churning as the crew alighted and took out their cameras. The palm trees were bending in the wind.

"If the storm gets too bad we're going for cover," Jack said.

"Fine by me," she said, then checked her makeup before she left the car. As she stepped out, the storm seemed to take on a life of its own. It swept the hood off her head. She grabbed it and closed the snap beneath her neck.

They quickly got the satellite connection to the feeder station. The rain began to pour again, just as the commentator from the D.C. station introduced her. Kimberly was drenched when the viewers got their first glimpse of her.

"Thanks, Joe. The wind and rain have increased significantly from yesterday. Hurricane Brighton is now three hours offshore. We're standing on the south shore of the island. The hotel and cabanas are on higher ground, and we're hoping the buildings won't be flooded."

"This is a popular tourist area, isn't it, Kimberly? How are they preparing for the storm?" the announcer asked.

"Yes, Joe. Most of the hotel guests left early, but a few hardy ones have decided to stay. The restaurant has plenty of food stocked. And all of the trash cans, chairs and umbrellas have been cleared from the beach," Kimberly said. After answering a few more questions, she prepared for the closing.

"Live at Canter Island, I'm Kimberly Canter. Now, Joe, back to you."

They had already filmed many of the islanders evacuating earlier that morning. The limbs from trees were already touching the ground.

"Another readout from the weather station, Kim," Jonas, her producer, said. "It looks like the hurricane season is off to an extra-early start, and this hurricane is coming closer to the island than first predicted. You may get a direct hit."

"I was afraid of that." A *direct hit* was the last thing Kimberly wanted to hear. She wished Jack had gotten on that plane.

Chapter 5

As the storm raged outside, Kimberly's emotions raged as strongly within.

She interviewed Devin and several guests who'd opted to stay, and gave a couple more news bites on the beach, with the wind rocking her, before she and Jack dashed into the hotel.

Since the hotel was designed to withstand hurricane-force winds, they felt safe holing up there. The porter had already transferred their luggage from the cabin to the hotel, and by the time they made it to their room, they were both dripping wet and cold. The maid had already filled the tub with water for when the electricity went out.

They quickly discarded their clothing, toweled off

and dressed in warm, dry clothes, before sliding under the covers to warm up.

Jack's gaze lingered on his wife.

Kimberly loved her job—and she was dedicated to it, as dedicated as he was to his brewpubs.

That was front and center in Jack's mind as they regarded each other with no more than a foot of space separating them. Still breathing raggedly, they fought to bring their breath under control.

Jack's emotions were raw and sharp. Kimberly's eyes were bright—and drawing closer to each other seemed as natural as breathing.

He wanted—needed—to imprint himself on her. It was a battle of wills of who would make the first move. Jack knew it would be him, but right now he wanted to luxuriate in watching her chest rise and fall with each quick breath.

Kimberly inched closer, took Jack's face between her hands and kissed him hard on the mouth. Immediately opening his lips, he thrust his tongue inside her mouth, deepening the kiss to breathtaking intensity. Capturing her hips, he brought her body flush with his. Her heartbeat hammered against his chest, blending with the staccato beat of his own.

He tore his mouth from hers. "You loved being out there in the raw elements, didn't you? Woman against nature."

Jack shifted on top of her, blending his strength with her softness. She was wild and unrestrained beneath him, as if heated from within. As raw as the raging storm outside, her fingers dug into his back, dragged lower until she clamped his butt cheeks with both hands, moving her hips, grinding against him through the impediment of their clothes.

"Got to slow down, baby, or I won't last," Jack whispered, his voice strained with need.

"I don't care. I need you—*now*, Jack."

Damn, she was hot and wild beneath him. But he wanted, needed, her hotter.

Kimberly ran her hands along his corded back, up to his chest.

Jack nuzzled her neck. From their long history, he knew she was extremely sensitive there, and he took his time giving her attention. Kimberly moaned with pleasure, spurred him to give her other delights.

He raked the blouse off her shoulders and tossed it aside, but paused when he discovered the bra hook was in back. He saw that as an opportunity, not an impediment.

Moving aside, he flipped Kimberly over, unhooked the bra, sliding it apart and down her arms, taking the time to layer a carpet of kisses along her back and arms, following every sensuous curve and line.

"Hmm…" A long, guttural moan ripped from Kimberly's throat, and she arched her spine when he dipped his tongue into the small of her back.

"Do you like that?"

"Sooo, so good," she whimpered, clenching the sheet in her fingers.

"You don't know the half of it," Jack said, as with long, loving strokes, he reached beneath her, unsnapped her pants. She lifted her hips to ease the way.

He unzipped them and the erotic scrape of the zipper sang a song of its own. He slid her pants, with her thong, down her hips and thighs, until she was completely naked.

For several sensual heartbeats he gazed upon the beautiful lines of her body. Then he stroked her buttocks and squeezed the tight muscles.

Jack spread her thighs apart, squeezing the muscles there, too, before he stroked the inside of her thigh. She moved to his loving beat as he pleasured her with kisses and sweet licks of his tongue, working from the outside to the inner thigh.

"God, yes... Jack, you're driving me insane," she moaned as his hand stroked her intimately, but only for a second. When he started to withdraw, she closed her legs around him. "No... No, don't go..." But he brushed her thighs apart once again, noticing a slight tremble.

"I'm just getting started, baby."

"Jack..."

He alternated nibbling kisses and licks all the way down her thighs, knees, calves, luxuriating in her sweet cries of pleasure before he flipped her over again.

Kimberly was so hot and so erotically alive, desire spread through every limb, every fiber, every cell, so intensely she thought she'd burst into searing flames. She reached for Jack, but he pulled back.

"Not yet, darling," he said, his voice rough with his own need and the need to take Kimberly higher. The look of intense desire on her face was a portrait worth painting, worth saving.

"Do you trust me, baby?" he asked, his expression so serious, Kimberly wondered at it.

"Of…of course," she said on a shaky breath.

Kimberly rose up to kiss him, but he used his lips to tease her around the edge of her mouth, over her lips, never lingering in one place long enough for her to capture him. Her tongue came out to touch his, but he would not insert his tongue into her mouth or capture hers in his. It was a duel of tongues mating—dancing, playful—before he drew a line on her cheeks, her chin, her neck and collarbone, until he finally shifted, then kissed her deeply, his tongue sucking gently, exploring the texture of her mouth. Kimberly slipped her hand beneath his shirt, desperate to feel the corded muscles and sprinkling of hair on his chest. She followed the line down to his pants, unbuttoned, unzipped. He was rock hard, and when she wrapped her hand around his considerable length she elicited a deep moan that caused the fire already burning in her stomach to flare in delight.

He pressed against her stomach, slid his hand lower before slipping a finger inside her. She moaned, moving her hips to press closer to his touch.

Their lovemaking bordered on desperation. An attempt to hold on to a relationship that was quickly disintegrating. Jack wanted the experience stamped in their memories for a lifetime.

If they could communicate in no other way, they spoke the same language in bed. Unresolved issues dissolved with a touch.

Kimberly ran her hands up his arms and around his

neck, pressing his mouth tighter against her own. Jack moaned deep in his throat, eliciting a deep-seated desire that spiraled out of control.

Kissing his neck as she slid her hands over his collarbone and down to his chest, she gathered his shirt in her hands and slid it up his chest. But he stopped her from removing it.

In the waning light, Jack leaned back to study her. Her breasts had swelled, her areolae darkened, her nipples were erect. He trailed his tongue around one areola, slowly working his way to the peak.

Kimberly held her breath, eagerly anticipating, as his lips began to move closer to the tip of her nipple. When he suckled gently on her tight bud it sent waves of pleasure to the center of her body.

"You are so beautiful," he said.

"Oh, Jack…Jack…" she moaned, his name a song on her lips, as he went from one breast to the other. Then he began a heated trail down to her abdomen, dipping a tongue in her navel before he worked his way farther down. The muscles in her thighs clenched with anticipation, and by the time he kissed her intimately, Kimberly was trembling with need. He licked and suckled her there, her desire building to mind-exploding proportions before he turned his head to layer nibbling kisses on her inner thigh, kissing her intimately once again, back and forth, until Kimberly screamed.

"You're driving me crazy," she cried.

He covered her completely with his mouth, seducing her with the warmth of his lips.

He stroked her with the moist softness of his

tongue while his hands caressed her tenderly. The pleasure built until she exploded with an orgasm that rivaled the storm outside.

Kimberly dragged in a ragged breath. Jack hovered beside her, stroking her tenderly, but as soon as her strength returned, she pressed him flat on the bed. "It's my turn," she said, as she slowly undressed him the rest of the way, springing teasing kisses on him.

She paid homage to every part of his body, giving him the pleasure he had so lovingly sprinkled on her. His guttural moans rippling in the air were heady and almost unreal. It wasn't until she was assured he was hot almost beyond endurance that she took mercy on him. But by that time, Jack snatched control back and tumbled her flat on her back, then slowly, slowly filled her with himself. Her body curled around him, accepting, urging him to make magic.

"Are you ready for me, sweetheart?" he growled, holding himself still above her.

"Yes, yes. Oh, yes…"

Rain pounded the windows as Jack pumped inside her. The roar of the thunder matched the thunderous beat of his heart. Quick lightning strikes flashed across the beauty of Kimberly's passion-glazed face, and the mighty wind matched the rush of her breath against his neck as it gushed out while the orgasm rocked them both to the core.

Completely limp, they lay side by side in a tangle of limbs, attempting to catch their breath.

As soon as reality resurfaced, they noticed the driving rain and wind against the windows and balcony.

"We'd better get dressed," Jack said, "or that window might explode and catch us naked."

"Wouldn't that be a story for the press?" Kimberly said, laughing. "Oh, crap. I have to go back on air." She washed at the sink, then dressed hurriedly and rushed out of the room.

They called the children that night. Sunday dawned, and Kimberly went with her crew to do a couple of news bites on the aftermath of the storm.

There was wave damage. Downed palms were all over the place. Some bushes had been uprooted, but the real worry was the relentless rain that dumped on the island. The hotel and cabanas didn't get flooded. The pool deck was littered with torn-up bushes and debris.

It was Monday morning before they caught a flight back to Washington. They took the water taxi across the choppy sea to the main island. Kimberly's already queasy stomach roiled with tension. She sat still, trying to keep her breakfast down. Sighing with relief when they finally made it without incident, she gladly climbed out of the boat, planting her feet on solid ground.

The main island suffered no more than a tropical storm, not nearly as bad as Canter Island. The rain had been heavy but not bad enough to uproot anything or damage buildings. There was some flooding, and sandbags were piled up so the water wouldn't overflow into the town.

Jack hailed a taxi, and they bounced on rutted roads, passing luxury hotels and middle-class houses and the town proper before they made it to the small airport on the outskirts of town.

When their flight finally took off, Kimberly rested her head against the headrest. She felt a change in their relationship but couldn't summon the energy to worry. Still, they'd be together for hours, and Kimberly used that time as an opportunity to talk, to clear the air before they returned home to life as usual.

"Jack, I love my job and I'm not going to quit it."

"I know you do. I saw your joy while you were on the air. It's different from watching you on TV."

"I'm not selfish. If I thought quitting my job would change anything between us, I would, but I don't think my job is the problem."

"I was wrong to ask you to quit. It would be like you asking me to quit working at the brewpubs."

"So…where does that leave us?" she asked.

Jack didn't respond.

"What happened to us? My work was never an issue before. You've always supported me."

Jack shook his head. "I still support you. But we seem to have gone in different directions. And I know, with you working full-time and I can't cut my hours, we'll never see each other."

Kimberly regarded him a moment. It was true they needed more time together. But she didn't see that happening, even if she cut her hours.

But something was missing. When they were in bed, all was perfect. But they couldn't live their lives between the sheets. When two people loved each other without reserve... She couldn't help but wonder what happened to make them lose their connection.

She had none of the answers. She didn't know how they'd begun to lose what made them special. And she was sick to death of thinking and talking about it.

If Kimberly had worked full-time all these years, she'd be the lead forecaster for the station by now. It wasn't going to happen working part-time. But her longevity gave her some perks, even at part-time.

"I'll ask the station to find someone willing to job-share with me again. The arrangement I had before worked well. Don't you agree?"

Jack nodded.

"Does that solve everything?" She knew it didn't, knew it was what he wanted to hear.

Jack gazed at his hand rubbing her thigh, and his gaze narrowed. "I think so. At least it's a start."

"The children still need you, Jack. This can't be one-sided."

"Even if I was around more, I wouldn't see them. They're always busy with their own interests."

"But they still need to see us working as a cohesive unit. They need to see us together sometimes. And we still need to do things with them in addition to the fifteen minutes they spend with you for breakfast, in addition to school activities. You have to participate in their lives."

Jack leaned over and kissed her. He, too, was unsure of the solution.

Jack's conversations with Kimberly weighed heavily on his mind. She'd made concessions in her

An Important Message from the Publisher

Dear Reader,

Because you've chosen to read one of our fine novels, I'd like to say "thank you"! And, as a special way to say thank you, I'm offering to send you two more Kimani™ Romance novels and two surprise gifts – absolutely FREE! These books will keep it real with true-to-life African American characters that turn up the heat and sizzle with passion.

Please enjoy the free books and gifts with our compliments...

Linda Gill

Publisher, Kimani Press

off Seal and
Place Inside...

EDITOR'S
FREE GIFTS
SEAL
THANK YOU

THE EDITOR'S "THANK YOU"
FREE GIFTS INCLUDE:

Two Kimani™ Romance Novels
Two exciting surprise gifts

YES! I have placed my Editor's "thank you" Free Gifts seal in the space provided at right. Please send me 2 FREE books, and my 2 FREE Mystery Gifts. I understand that I am under no obligation to purchase anything further, as explained on the back of this card.

PLACE
FREE GIFTS
SEAL
HERE

DETACH AND MAIL CARD TODAY!

168 XDL EVGW

368 XDL EVJ9

FIRST NAME

LAST NAME

ADDRESS

APT.#

CITY

STATE / PROV.

ZIP/POSTAL CODE

Thank You!

(K-R3M-09)

career to please him. He could do no less. The Friday after their vacation, he got off early and left Lauren to take up the slack.

He'd had a couple of meetings scheduled that afternoon and had had his secretary reschedule one of them. He'd also planned to run by a couple of his pubs that evening. Fridays were always busy.

Earlier that week he'd asked the children to plan an activity they could participate in together over the weekend.

They'd looked at him in puzzlement, as if he'd drank too much of his own beer. Had he completely lost touch with them?

Although he knew he should have made arrangements earlier in the day, he'd called Kimberly an hour ago to see if she wanted him to bring dinner home, but she didn't answer her cell phone. She might have been taking a nap so she could stay up later that evening. He brought dinner home anyway.

Maybe this could be an olive branch. It still cut deep that she thought he was a neglectful husband and father. His dad worked hard. How could she expect less of him? This was what a man was supposed to do. How many women did he hear complaining that the men didn't do enough?

When he got home no one was there. He tried dialing Byron's phone number.

"Yeah, Dad?" His son sounded rushed. There was a lot of noise in the background, as if he were at a game or something. Jack didn't think there was a game today.

"What time will you be getting home? I thought we'd play a little miniature golf this evening, or take in a movie. Make it a family evening." The children hadn't come up with anything, and miniature golf was something they all could do. The temperature was comfortable enough.

"I'm at the game, Dad."

"I'll pick up April and bring her. Maybe we can do something afterward."

"The game will be over by the time you get here. It's a couple hours away."

"Oh. Well, I'll hunt down April and your mother. Maybe we can wait for you. What time do you think you'll get home?" Jack asked.

"I don't know. It'll be late. Mom's on her way here with April. There's an outlet out here somewhere. They mentioned doing some shopping," he said, as if rushed. "The JV game is first, but they should get here soon."

Jack heard someone calling Byron in the background. "Yeah, yeah. Okay," he heard his son shout before he came back to the phone.

"Gotta go, Dad."

Before Jack could wish him good luck, the connection broke and all he heard was the jarring beeping in his ear.

Jack closed the phone slowly. He smelled the food loaded on the countertop, but he wasn't really hungry. He should have called Kimberly ahead of time, he thought once again. His gaze traveled to the white board calendar attached to the fridge. The game was scribbled in bold blue letters. The house was quiet and unsettling.

Clearly, there was no sense hanging around when there was plenty of work to be done. After storing the food in the fridge, Jack headed for his car and pointed it toward the office.

Maybe he'd make it back by the time Kimberly and the children arrived.

Lauren was there when he arrived.

She glanced up from her computer screen.

"I thought you were turning in early," he said.

"I thought you were."

"Everybody's occupied." He ran a hand across his head. Maybe Kimberly had a point. He did see more of Lauren than he saw of her. But he never even contemplated a relationship with the woman. She was an employee, for God's sake.

"I've been thinking that maybe I'm too hands-on. I need to take more of a backseat and work on acquiring more space for pubs. The locations we have so far have worked extremely well." Another of Kimberly's complaints.

"It will make your GMs happy. They're very qualified, you know."

Jack frowned. "Make them happy? Are they displeased about something?"

Lauren shrugged. "They have mentioned that you are a little *too* hands-on. Always underfoot, as if you don't trust them."

"If I didn't trust them, I wouldn't have hired them."

"I know."

"But?"

"I don't want to lose my job. I love working here,

and it isn't often that you find a job that suits you as well as this one suits me."

A flicker of concern crossed his brow. "Feel free to talk. I'm not going to fire you for speaking your mind."

"You've got a great setup. And I wish you didn't feel that you needed to triple-check everything I do. I've been here for months. I've worked in brewpubs before and I know my job."

"I know that."

"There's a paper trail for everything. You don't have to be as hands-on as you are. You can let your managers do the job you pay us to do. Which would leave more time for you to make acquisitions so that you can grow this company as large as you want to. That was the reason you hired me, and I don't think you're utilizing me to my full potential."

For a moment, Jack wanted to fire her on the spot. It was his damn company, and if he wanted to triple-check everything, he had every right to. He'd built it from the ground up. Lauren was still in school when he started out. But he pulled back. He could take constructive criticisms.

"I've upset you," Lauren said. "I hope you aren't about to fire me." Lauren's brows furrowed in concern. Jack could tell she already regretted saying anything.

"I'm not going to fire you. I want you to feel free to discuss your concerns," he said. Lauren wasn't just a good worker. She was great at her job. "I'll think about what you've said. But remember, the ultimate decision is mine."

"Of course."

Jack made his way to his office. Was he really so bad that his employees were complaining behind his back? Most of them had been with him for years and hadn't made one complaint to his face.

Sitting at his desk, he stared at the picture of Kimberly and the children. He thought about her, too, and all her demands of late. Was he that out of tune with the people around him?

They'd been back one week and it didn't take long for Kimberly's office to find someone to job-share with her. The woman was a new mother, and a seasoned on-air personality for a sister station in Cincinnati. Her husband had accepted a DJ slot on a popular Washington radio station. Like Kimberly, she enjoyed her job but wanted to spend some time with her baby. It wasn't easy getting up at two, five mornings a week.

But it would be at least a month before she arrived.

The only reason Kimberly had accepted the full-time position was because the children were leaving, not to mention it gave her more of a chance for a promotion.

She'd had high hopes that if she revealed her concerns about their marriage, Jack would make a change. That certainly hadn't happened, but working fewer hours made sense. *Somebody* needed to be home *some* of the time.

Kimberly was pleased that Jack was making an effort. They'd even had dinner together a couple of times and he had actually attended one of Byron's games. Kimberly was very pleased. After dinner she showered. Jack was knotting his tie when she came out of the bathroom.

"Good news," she said as she rubbed on lotion.

"What?" he asked. Her gaze met his in the mirror.

"They found someone to job-share with me."

"When does this happen?"

"In a month. We'll work alternating two- and three-day weeks. And you'll see more of me than you want." She kissed him on the cheek and began to apply her makeup.

"Great."

She peered at him closely. "You don't sound too enthusiastic."

"I'm pleased."

They'd made plans to see a play in D.C. This was what she wanted. Time to do things with her husband. She'd left the Caribbean with little hope, but he'd changed. Byron told her Jack had called him earlier that week with the intent of attending his game. Jack really had listened. After she dressed, Kimberly approached Jack and kissed him again. He smiled, linking his arms around her.

"Keep this up and we'll skip the play."

Kimberly playfully pinched his side. "Not on your life, mister."

The Tyler Perry play was as entertaining as always. Kimberly couldn't remember when she'd last laughed so much.

"Thanks, Jack," she said as they walked out of the theater.

He grasped her hand and smiled, then pulled her close and wrapped an arm around her shoulder.

The traffic was light on the drive home. Kimberly almost wished it was like the old days, when she could sit close on a bench seat.

They made it home in record time and went upstairs to undress.

"Well, the kids are away, so we can play," Kimberly said, sticking her leg out playfully, running it up and down his leg as they changed clothes. Jack had always liked her legs, and he'd already peeled down to his briefs.

"You look different," he said.

Kimberly frowned. "How?"

Jack shrugged. "I don't know. Just different."

"Humph. Different good or bad?" she asked.

"Not bad, just… I don't know."

"Are you ready for bed or do you want to watch a movie or listen to music?" she asked, peering in the mirror to see if she detected a change. She certainly hadn't gained weight. With her regular exercise routine, she was still the size eight she'd been for years. And her clothing certainly didn't fit any tighter.

"Not really. I guess I'll take a shower." But he didn't move.

"I can pop some popcorn, like old times. Maybe I'll even do the root beer float."

"Whatever."

Kimberly's good mood was quickly deteriorating. "If you're tired, I can give you a massage," she said.

"Umm. I'm not in the mood."

"Maybe a hot shower would revive you, or we can go to bed," Kimberly said. "We don't have to do anything."

She pulled on shorts and a sleeveless T-shirt and went downstairs. As she took an apple out of the fruit bowl she noticed Jack still hadn't turned on the shower. She started to bite into the fruit when she heard the doorbell ring.

When she approached the door, she heard Jack's feet pounding down the steps. For someone so tired, he certainly got an energy burst. Curious, Kimberly made it to the door first and opened it.

"Hi, Lauren," Kimberly said, frowning.

"Hi, Kimberly. Is Jack here?"

"Right here," Jack said, coming up behind her. He even wore a smile on his face. He had perked up since she left him stewing in the bedroom.

"Come in," Kimberly said, moving back to let the other woman enter.

"I won't be but a minute," she said, crossing the threshold. She was dressed in black tight pants and a mauve shirt. Kimberly didn't wear clothes that tight to work.

Kimberly led her to the family room. "I just came by to drop off some papers," she said to Jack. "How was the meeting?"

"Better than I thought," Jack said. "They're going to make a decision in the next couple of weeks."

"May I get you something to drink, Lauren?" Kimberly asked.

"No, thank you."

Kimberly left the room. She hoped they weren't discussing another acquisition. She'd clearly let Jack know she was against it.

Lauren stayed for ten minutes. When she left, Kimberly approached Jack.

"What was that all about that it couldn't wait until Monday?"

Jack sighed. "I'm buying another brewpub."

"I thought you weren't going to open another one right now," she said.

"This is too good to turn down," he said.

"This is the first night we've spent together in ages. It'll stop as soon as you acquire another pub."

"This is important," he said impatiently.

"We're important, Jack. I thought you understood. I've given up a chance at a promotion because you asked me to. The least you could do is make some concession for this marriage, too. It can't be all one-sided."

"I was a father at twenty-two. I had dreams of traveling around, doing the things young college graduates do before I settled down, but you were pregnant and I fell into the role of husband and father. Now I have other goals that I don't want to sacrifice."

"And you feel like you've missed out on life? That I caused you to sacrifice these dreams?"

Jack rubbed a hand over his face. "I don't want to hurt you. I love you and the kids… It's not about you. It's me."

"Are you trying to say that you don't want to be here with me anymore?" Kimberly asked, feeling the bottom drop out of her stomach. This shouldn't be a surprise. She'd seen the writing on the wall, but hadn't wanted to believe it.

"What about the children?" Kimberly asked, realizing nothing had changed. "You only see them in the mornings now. You attended one game. You don't participate in other activities with them. You're always gone, and that won't change with opening another brewpub," Kimberly said. "How does Lauren fit into this?"

"She's an employee. Nothing more."

"Who you're attracted to."

"I have a hard-and-fast rule that I don't date employees. I've never broken that rule, especially not with Lauren."

"But you want to."

"I didn't say that."

"You didn't deny it either." When he remained silent, Kimberly said, "Jack, if I'm not the woman you want to be with any longer, if you feel this relationship is stifling you, then maybe you should move out and apply for a divorce."

"Kim…Kim, I never said I want a divorce." He threw up his hands. "I don't know what I want. And I certainly didn't mean to hurt you, but I'm sick to death of your complaining. It's wearing me out. And it's unnecessary."

"It's called communication. Something we don't seem to do very much anymore. Don't you think not knowing if you want another woman would hurt me?"

"You're blowing everything out of proportion. I still love you."

"I've made a sacrifice."

"Kim…"

"I don't make enough money to live off now. You

even wanted me to quit my job—quit my job, when you knew all along you were going to buy that brew-pub. You lied to me."

"Not intentionally." Jack swept a hand across his face. "I can't talk to you anymore," he said. "You know you'll never have to worry about money."

"I don't know any such thing. Wife number two won't like the fact that money she could use is going to wife number one."

"You're blowing this way out of proportion. I'm not even seeing another woman."

Kimberly turned, headed to the stairs.

"Kim…"

"You acted like I was the reason our marriage was in jeopardy, while all the time you were making plans without discussing them with me. I want you to pack your bags and leave. Now."

"Kim…"

She wasn't listening as she ran upstairs. Her world had turned on its axis.

It was a good thing the kids were spending the night elsewhere, because Kimberly couldn't deal with them tonight.

Kimberly pulled jeans over her shorts, grabbed her keys and left. She drove to an almost-empty parking lot and cried until she had no more tears.

Jack hadn't expected this. He felt like somebody had smacked him with a two-by-four. His first impulse was to stop Kimberly as she ran past him, but he didn't know what to say. He hated like hell to hurt her. And he knew he had. But could he keep lying to her and himself? She was being so unreasonable.

And he certainly wasn't attracted to Lauren. He didn't want a divorce. He never expected her to ask for one. It was… Damn it, he was just confused right now. Couldn't a man go through changes without the world coming to an end? Women used the excuse of their PMS. Men had nothing to use as an excuse except "middle-age crazy." But he hadn't hit middle age yet.

For the past few months he'd been plagued with a sense of unfulfilled ambition and achievement. He felt as if he was standing still as life was passing him by.

He should be on top of the world. He had two wonderful children, a wonderful wife, a house big enough for three families and enough money to satisfy his wildest dream. But he worked so hard he didn't have time for dreams. And suddenly, all the things he had, which were blessings really, didn't seem to be enough.

Yet, he couldn't envision his life without Kimberly. He felt a deep sense of abiding loss.

And his kids. How could he walk out on his children? He loved them with every beat of his heart.

Jack sat for several minutes. He didn't have to leave forever. Maybe he and Kimberly needed a short separation. He needed some time to pull his thoughts together.

Jack went upstairs, pulled out a suitcase and packed enough clothes to last a week. He shouldn't be gone longer than that.

Chapter 6

Two days later, Jack dialed April's cell phone but got no response. Five times more he dialed it as he drove to his house—or what used to be his home. He was still miffed at Kimberly and didn't want to go inside to see her. Just the sight of her was enough to piss him off. Throwing him out of his own home! And now he was thrown into the role of some stranger—some trespasser. Well, he wasn't going to ring the doorbell to his own damn house.

Damn it. Jack parked his car in the driveway and climbed out. He wondered if his usual place in the garage was empty, or if Kimberly had filled it up with junk.

Using his key, he let himself into the house. It was

as quiet as a tomb. He strolled to the kitchen to see if April was there and came up short.

Kimberly's head was under the sink and her well-shaped behind, covered with red shorts, was poking up in the air. Jack frowned. The shorts were way too short. He could see her butt cheeks. He smothered a moan of desire, dragging in a deep breath to cool his ardor, before reluctantly tearing his gaze from her butt to the various tools stacked on the floor. A book was held open with a wrench.

With a disgruntled sigh, he reminded himself she put him out. He was not going to be the one to give in this time.

"What are you doing?" he asked.

He heard a bump, then a curse. Kimberly's head snapped out and she was rubbing it. "What are you doing here?" she asked accusingly.

"April called. Said she needed some supplies. She said you were out. You okay?"

"I'm fine," she said.

He studied her stubborn features. "I thought you got all the supplies at the beginning of the school year."

"I can't plan for everything."

He nodded toward the sink. "What are you doing?"

"The sink's stopped up, so I'm taking it apart."

"Why didn't you just call a plumber?" he asked, knowing well Kimberly wasn't handy at mechanical things.

"Because now that I'm a single woman I have to learn to do the repairs. I can't call a plumber every time something breaks down."

Jack gritted his teeth. "You're not single. And you know I would have paid for the plumber. We still share bank accounts."

"For how long?"

"Don't be any more difficult than you already are," he snapped. He was at the end of his patience with her.

Kimberly stuck her head back underneath the cabinet. "April should be upstairs. Why don't you go look for her?"

Jack muttered an oath and paced over to the sink. "Move over."

"I have it," she snapped.

"No, you don't. You've never repaired a sink in your life. Honestly, you're the most stubborn woman I've ever met." He physically hauled her from beneath the sink and set her aside, all but tossing her.

"I didn't ask you to fix it."

He didn't say a word as he went to work on the sink. Five minutes later, he pulled a huge wad of what looked like celery strings and a couple of mangled toothbrushes out of the drain and threw a suspicious look at Kimberly.

"How did all this get in there?"

"How would I know? I have more sense than to put good food or toothbrushes in the disposal."

A noise by the door drew Jack's gaze. April stood there looking sheepish.

"We're going to have a talk, young lady."

"I didn't mean to, Dad. I forgot to tell Mom the toothbrushes slipped out of my hand when I was pulling new ones out of the box. The phone rang and I forgot about it after I answered it."

Sure she did, Jack thought, disappearing back under the sink to secure the elbow joint back in place. April had disappeared by the time he finished, and so had Kimberly.

He stacked the tools and carried them out to the garage, storing them in their proper places. Kimberly always had to take things to the extreme—and leave things where he couldn't find them again.

Back inside, he climbed the stairs to April's room. She was lying across the bed, crying her pitiful heart out.

Jack felt devastated for her. He sat beside her and gathered her into his arms. "It's okay, baby. I fixed the sink."

"I want you to come home, Daddy. I don't want you and Mama to get a divorce."

"Who said anything about a divorce? Your mom and I just need some time apart to think. Your old man is still here, sweetheart. Now get cleaned up so I can take you out."

When his daughter dashed to her bathroom, Jack glanced at the door to see Kimberly standing there. Her face was as sad as their daughter's.

She'd lost weight. She wasn't that big to begin with. Why didn't she just come to her senses, relent and ask him to come home? She glanced away from him.

Why was she even putting them through this ridiculous ordeal?

With every breath in her body, Kimberly wanted to ask Jack to move back. But she couldn't continue to live the way things were. She'd bargained for a live-in husband, not an absentee one.

April's tears had ripped through her like a shredder, tearing her insides to pieces. It took everything in her not to cry herself. She didn't want to do this to the children. Even though she was nineteen when her parents announced their separation, it had still hurt. It had still felt as if something vital had been ripped from her.

And watching Jack interact with April. Oh, Lord, why couldn't he be there on a daily basis? Why did disaster have to strike before he participated?

Tearing her gaze from the heart-wrenching scene, Kimberly ran downstairs. Her stomach felt hollow because she hadn't been eating. But she still couldn't seem to gather up the energy to eat. She knew she'd lost some weight. Her clothes were feeling loose on her. Even her makeup person had commented on it. She had to eat something or she'd make herself sick.

Kimberly opened the fridge and did what she told her children a million times not to do. Letting the cold air escape, she stared at the contents inside.

Jack had moved out only days ago, and Kimberly already felt bereft. An unrelenting fist squeezed her heart. People who said love didn't hurt had never been in love. Her chest felt as if an elephant had sat upon it and taken up residence.

The kids were moping around the house, especially April, who was alternating with bouts of tears. She was definitely Daddy's girl. Kimberly had to carry on as if everything would be all right, when she felt as if her world would never be right again.

She made an appointment for her yearly gynecological checkup and thought she'd also make an appointment with her regular physician for a prescription to help her sleep. In the past, she always slept like a rock, and she never thought the day would come when she'd need help.

If she didn't start sleeping at night, she'd soon look like the walking dead. As it was, the makeup artist had to use extra makeup. The man had even commented on her appearance.

"Girlfriend, what is wrong with you? You're not getting enough?"

He'd never felt the liberty of commenting on her sex life before. It was not something she would discuss in her work environment.

But she'd nearly burst into tears. With much effort, she'd held the waterworks at bay while he rambled on about his latest conquest. Good thing he could go on for hours without her responding. Some people just loved to hear themselves talk.

It was almost the end of May, and tonight was her son's last baseball game. As usual, she'd be his only parent there.

She drove to the school. It was her night to work the concession stand during intermission. Several of the parents stopped by to talk while she served up chili dogs, nachos, pizza, hamburgers, sodas and candy.

Then the game started. She got a few minutes' break until intermission. Her son's team was winning by one run.

While she was serving, Jack arrived. She did a double take. Jack never appeared at the games.

She was acutely aware of his tall, athletic physique, and the outline of his broad shoulders inside the green polo shirt. Since it was cool, he wore a windbreaker over it. Which didn't stop her from focusing on the jeans that molded to him. Unfortunately, he stood close enough to her that the light aroma of his soap teased her senses. She wanted to take him to bed that moment. Have mercy. What in the world was she going to do?

She'd done everything but stand on her head to get Jack to attend games, and he always put her off because he was too busy. *And now that we're separated, he appears for his son's game.* Would she ever understand him?

"Hello, Kim," Jack said. His dark eyes watched her like a hawk, and she found his presence disturbing in ways that were going to get her into trouble.

She summoned up a smile. "Jack. What can I get you?" A line was forming behind him, so maybe he'd move on quickly.

He gazed deeply into her eyes, but she broke contact. "A bottle of water, please."

She handed him the water, but instead of taking it, his hand wrapped around hers. The coolness from the bottle pressed against one side, but heat from his hand pressed against the other. She felt as if she was on fire. Suddenly, he released her and she snatched her hand back, hoping it wasn't shaking when she took his money.

"Hi, Mom," April piped up with a smile, coming up behind her father.

Kimberly sucked in a breath and pasted what she

hoped was a natural smile on her face. "Hi, honey."
Kimberly knew she looked foolish. She felt conspicu-
ous. But after the exchange with Jack she couldn't get
herself under control. The little imp had gotten her
dad to bring her here. *Little Miss Matchmaker,*
Kimberly thought sadly. April wanted them back
together, and this was one of her tactics. Kim hated that
the children were so unhappy, but she didn't know
what to do to reach Jack.

He was still standing there. Kimberly wished he
would just go to the stands.

Jack couldn't deny that Kimberly looked lovely. He
knew he shouldn't have clamped his hand around hers,
but he wanted to touch her. She wore jeans, but still...

"I want nachos and a Pepsi," April announced. "Can
you buy it for me, Daddy?"

"Make that water, young lady," her mother said.

April let out a long sigh. "I don't know why you're
on this health kick."

Kimberly handed over the water and nachos and
Jack paid for them.

"How're they playing?" he found himself asking.

"Up by one."

Jack nodded, and with the bottle of water in his
hand, he followed April to the stands.

After the initial rush of trying to get his first two
pubs going, Jack had made it to a few soccer games,
to ballet and piano recitals. But as the years passed,
he'd bought more pubs, and things got too busy at
work again. He'd let Kimberly take care of the events.

But his daughter was requiring more of his time. His sister had picked her up from school and dropped her off at his office. April had convinced him to have dinner with her and had dragged him to the game. She had an entire schedule of events lined up for him. Even if he wanted to date another woman, which he didn't, he couldn't.

She'd never been this clingy before, never required this much of his time. Before the separation, breakfast was all she required of him. But now that he wasn't at the house, he worried that she wasn't eating a proper breakfast before she went off to school. Maybe he should at least keep up that part of their routine. Kimberly wouldn't be there in the mornings. And the kids still needed him.

He swiped a hand across his face. He didn't know what was going on with them any longer. Why couldn't they click? There was a time when they talked for hours without a break. They could spend the whole day, the two of them, and never run out of things to say and do. Suddenly, he didn't know his wife anymore. She just wasn't reasonable.

After a while, another woman took Kimberly's place at the snack bar. She went and sat with women she obviously knew. They made their very own cheering section. Something stirred in the pit of Jack's stomach. He didn't know any of these people. For too long he'd worked to make a living, but he hadn't been involved in his children's lives. They'd grown up without him.

When the game was over Jack approached Kimberly. "Did you get my suit from the cleaners?"

"No."

"Why not?"

"You don't live at home anymore. I don't take care of your clothes."

"Are you serious?"

She rolled her eyes at him and turned to speak to another parent.

"It's confirmed. You're pregnant," Kimberly's gynecologist said two weeks later.

The bottom dropped out of Kimberly's stomach. "Vicky, it can't be true." Only a month had gone by since her trip to the Caribbean. It seemed so much longer.

"You should be happy. You and Jack have been trying for years. And you can tell him to rest assured all his parts are in working order."

"And then some," Kimberly said before she could catch herself.

Vicky laughed, but Kimberly couldn't even begin to join her.

Kimberly sat as if struck speechless, and Vicky rubbed her arms.

"What's wrong?"

"Jack moved out."

"What? Dependable Jack?"

Kimberly nodded. "It's a long story."

"Well, I guess he better just move himself back in," Vicky said. "He wanted this child—and you shouldn't have to raise it alone."

"It's not that easy."

"Of course it is. I've got appointments rolling one after the other today. Sit for a few minutes and pull yourself together, then go home. I'll call you as soon as I finish up here and we'll go out to dinner."

"I can't eat."

"You have to eat. You're going to begin taking prenatal vitamins," she said. "Leave your cell phone on. I'll pick you up from your house." With a quick hug, Vicky left the room.

Kimberly dressed and, with the name of the prenatal vitamins in hand, made her way outside of the building, and on shaky legs struggled to a bench. Her head was swimming. It was absolutely impossible. No wonder she was feeling emotional. She was pregnant.

My God. Pregnant. Why now, when my marriage is failing?

She laughed out loud. Fate was a funny thing. Jack would be thrilled with the news.

It was a beautiful, sunny day, and the sun poured down on her, heating her from inside out.

God, she loved her children. She rubbed her stomach, even though it was too soon for her to show. Already, she loved this little one, too. What a blessing. But she couldn't help but think the timing was way off.

She couldn't tell Jack. He'd married her in the first place because she was pregnant. She knew that if she told him, he'd come back, and she didn't want a baby bringing him back this time. She wanted him only if he loved her and wanted to be with her.

Tears welled and ran down her cheeks. If hers and Jack's love wasn't strong enough to sustain the marriage, then she'd raise this child alone. She swiped the tears away. She loved Jack, but she could survive without him.

She stood, started to her car.

"Kim?"

Turning so fast that she almost tripped, she came face-to-face with Jonas, her producer.

"Are you okay?"

Kimberly forced herself to smile. "I'm great."

Her cell rang.

"Excuse me, Jonas," she said before she answered.

"Sorry, kiddo, but I have a delivery," Vicky said. "One of my patients has gone into labor. Are you going to be okay? There's no telling when I'll get there."

"I'm fine. Go deliver your baby."

Jonas seemed to study her. She knew she hadn't been in top form lately, and it was something he would have noticed.

She smiled brighter. "I'm fine, really."

He glanced at his watch. "It's almost five. Why don't we have dinner together? Or do you have other plans?"

She didn't have *any* plans. It was Jack's evening with the kids, so she'd only wander around the house alone. Maybe it would help if she got out. Jonas was safe.

What a shame. Men were scarce, and Jonas was a very nice guy and quite handsome, too. Women were always coming on to him. She'd told him more than once that he should "come out," but he wouldn't. He'd said some things weren't anybody's business. But he also said he never dated women. He wasn't into false pretenses.

"Let me go home and change first," Kimberly said.

"Shall I pick you up in an hour?"

"Sure," she said, looking forward to getting out for a change. The kids both had busy schedules this weekend. She'd told Byron to make sure April had rides to wherever she needed to go, just in case Jack had to work. *One of the few advantages of a teen with a driver's license,* she thought, as she headed home.

She showered and changed, spritzed on perfume and carefully applied her makeup. She hadn't dressed up since the night she and Jack went to the play together.

When Jonas picked her up he named a popular restaurant and drove directly there. It was crowded. But when she saw her husband there with Lauren and a couple of men, her stomach turned. They were probably discussing the new pub. Nausea threatened, but she swallowed. Jack wore a suit, not the brewpub shirt. He looked great. She gritted her teeth against the desire and anger vying for payback.

She just knew there was something going on between him and Lauren. That woman was after her husband, and now she undoubtedly felt he was free for the taking.

Fleetingly, Kimberly realized she was being irrational, but she was glad she'd dressed carefully for dinner. At least she wouldn't look like some pitiful thing waiting on the sidelines for Jack to make up his mind. And at least he'd think other men found her attractive. Jonas hadn't been at the station long, and Jack hadn't met him yet. He also didn't know Jonas was gay, and she wasn't about to tell him.

She made a point of not looking his way when they passed his table. Jonas said something to her and she laughed a little as she answered, hoping it didn't sound strained.

Jack couldn't believe it. What the heck was his wife doing, out with another man?

"Jack?" His name sounded as if it were coming from a long tunnel. He focused on Lauren for a second before he followed his wife's progress to a table. He had a perfect view of her. And, damn, she looked good. Frowning, he wondered if she wore his favorite perfume.

"Jack?"

"Oh, yeah," he said, focusing for a few seconds on the group. He'd ordered a nice steak and it was congealing in his stomach.

Lauren sighed. "What's wrong?"

"Nothing," he said, shaking his head. *If you don't count the fact that my wife is stepping out with another man.* Tearing his attention from his wife, Jack returned to the conversation.

Halfway through dinner, Kimberly went to the ladies' room. Jack excused himself and waited by the door for her to come out. He felt like a stalker.

"What do you think you're doing?" he asked, tugging her to the side.

She looked surprised to see him. "Oh, hi, Jack. How are you?"

"What the heck is going on, Kim?"

"I'm having dinner. Just like you."

"You're a married woman." She had worn his favorite perfume, and it set his temper ablaze. She was his, damn it. She had no business going out with another man.

"The fact that you're a married man hasn't stopped you from having dinner with other women." She lifted her chin, meeting his icy gaze straight on.

He wouldn't state the obvious, that there was a *group* of people at his table, not just Lauren. "What about the kids, Kim? They need parents now more than ever. Isn't that what you're always preaching to me? They search for all kinds of trouble at this age. April is having a hard time with the separation, and you're painting the town with another man," he all but spat.

"They're staying with you this weekend, remember? This should give you an opportunity to spend some quality time with them. To reassure April that you're still there for her."

Oh, crap. He'd forgotten about the weekend schedule. "You just remember you're still a married woman."

She tilted her chin. "Take your own advice, Jack. I have to get back to my table. Excuse me."

And just like that she took off, her hips swishing. Her skirt hem hit against her gorgeous legs. Her feet were encased in strappy, high-heeled sandals. He felt his body harden. Crimping his mouth, he took out his cell phone to call the kids.

His daughter started screeching in the phone. "Dad,

where are you? You were supposed to pick me up from Tracy's hours ago," she said accusingly.

"Where are you?"

"At home. My friend's mother dropped me off. What happened?"

"I got tied up. Baby, I'm sorry. I'm on my way."

At the table, he signaled for the waiter and paid the bill before hastening Lauren on her way. She was a bit put off, but what could he do? He couldn't help but notice Kimberly laughing and having a grand old time with her friend. He'd only had enough time to eat half of his dinner.

"Why are we rushing away?" Lauren asked.

"I forgot I was supposed to pick up my daughter. We have plans for the weekend."

"What a good dad you are," Lauren said.

"Not so good. I forgot to pick her up."

"You're a hardworking man. I'd think your wife could do that for you."

"She does more than her share," he said with a finality that let her know the subject was closed. What went on with his family was none of her business. But what he'd said was true.

Vicky arrived a half hour after Jonas dropped Kimberly off.

She plopped on the sofa. "Girl, I am beat. First-time mother, and the labor was long."

"What did she have?" Kimberly asked, a catch in her throat.

"A beautiful little girl," Vicky said with a sigh.

"You think they're all beautiful," Kimberly said. "And they're certainly precious."

"Especially that little one you're carrying. You need to tell Jack."

Kimberly sighed, the joy leaving. "I can't."

"Honey, in three more months you won't have to."

"Hopefully, we'll resolve our differences by then," Kimberly said.

"Or when you turn green and flash to the bathroom."

"He wouldn't know. He isn't home."

"I bet he notices more than you think."

"Let's talk about you. How was the date you had a week ago?"

Vicky shook her head. "I don't know why I waste my time. All these years, and I haven't found one— not one man—who clicked. I'm off them for a while."

"You can't close your eyes."

"Opening them does no good." She wagged a finger. "You better keep that man. It's not easy finding good ones."

"I've got the perfect one to introduce you to. He's really nice. Just your—"

Vicky held up a hand. "Stop it right there. I don't want to be fixed up. If we make plans for an evening out, I want to be able to relax—not hurt your feelings when it doesn't work out."

"But…"

"I mean it, Kim. No matchmaking. They never work out anyway."

"You are so stubborn."

"My advice to you is to hold on to Jack with any excuse you can. It'd be different if you didn't love each other."

Kimberly's sigh was long and painful. "I don't know that he does love me."

"You've been married for seventeen years. Something's there. You just have to find it."

"I don't know that we can. I'm tired of being the one to give in, to sacrifice, without him making an effort to do the same."

"Oh, Kim. Can't you find a way to talk through this problem?"

"Jack tells me one thing and does another. I'm not putting up with it anymore."

"Kim—"

"I don't want to weaken. I don't want to hold on to a man who really doesn't want me—who isn't sure I'm the one he wants to be with." Kimberly drew out a long breath. Then she sighed. "You know, even though he's rarely here, even though I rarely see him, I miss him."

"And I know he misses you, too."

Jack's sister Janice caught him in the parking lot. Before he could greet her, she bared down on him.

"How could you leave your wife?" she asked. Every inch of her five-four frame vibrated with rage and disappointment. At twenty-six, Janice was the youngest of his family.

He hadn't started this mess. "Who told you that?"

"Never mind. You're the one always haranguing us

about doing what's right. But here you are leaving a good wife."

"Stay out of it, Janice. You don't know what you're talking about. I can handle my business."

"Oh, really? We always suffered your advice, whether we wanted it or not. Big brother and all, sticking his nose in everybody's business. You think you're the only one who can give advice?"

"You can't advise on something you know nothing about," Jack snapped, quickly nearing the end of his patience.

"You are such an autocrat."

"You're a nosey busybody."

"Mama is upset. Tell *her* she's nosey. We all love Kimberly."

He knew that.

"I don't want to find out you left her for some hoochie mama."

"You won't." Had she been talking to Byron?

With hands on hips, she glared at him—but then she hugged him and got in her car and peeled away.

His wife had started a firestorm that was just beginning. That evening, Jack got a visit from his mother that didn't go any better than the visit with his sister. They all blamed him—and he couldn't tell them Kimberly put him out. Then they'd want to know what he'd done. Because of course it had to be his fault.

Women.

Chapter 7

"April, what time did Byron say he was bringing his date?" Byron had invited his very first serious girlfriend to dinner to introduce her to Kimberly. Kimberly touched a hand to her chest. She couldn't believe it. *Her baby.* Of course he was sixteen, so it was expected for him to experience his first bout of puppy love. But still, time passed just too quickly. Kimberly only hoped the girl was a nice young lady.

"In half an hour. But he's taking me to the store first, and then he's going to pick her up on the way back. I need some supplies for school."

"Honey, you have plenty of supplies you haven't even used up yet. Did you check the den to make sure? Just the other week your father had to take you to get supplies."

"I checked, Mom. It won't take but a few minutes."

"What is her name? That boy forgot to even mention a name."

"I don't know. Some strange name, like Akenda, or something like that."

"What an unusual name. Is she African?"

"How would I know?" April blew out a long breath and gazed up at the ceiling, as if her mother was lacking a few brain cells, then she grabbed candles from the cabinet and dashed into the dining room. Puzzled, Kimberly followed her.

The table was gorgeous, even without the candles. April had placed little bunches of cut roses around the candelabra, and now she placed a candle in each holder. The table was set with Kimberly's best china.

Kimberly frowned. She'd thought they'd be more relaxed, not scare the girl. "Honey, you don't think you're overdoing it a bit? You don't want to make the girl nervous. It's not a wedding celebration or Thanksgiving."

"It's been forever since we did anything special, Mom," April complained. "I thought we'd do it up really nice tonight. You used to do this all the time, remember? You'd play old-time, slow music. I found one of your old CDs and put it on. You know the ones Dad had made? Remember when he brought this huge bag of CDs home and you started doing old dances and acting silly?"

Kimberly remembered all right. Jack had just opened a new brewpub. The grand-opening weekend had been so successful that he was in a jovial mood. They'd danced. And the kids had watched a while, and then grew bored. She and Jack had snuggled up, she with a glass of wine, Jack with a tall beer. Kimberly breathed in deeply.

It was an evening to remember.

Kimberly worked to keep tears from spilling.

Bobbing double time to the beat, April danced around the table, inserting candles. "Seems like years ago since you really went way out," April said.

Kimberly sighed, guilt skirting around her conscience. "It has been a while, hasn't it? But this isn't for me," Kimberly warned. The child talked as if the music was from the thirties or something. "You might want to play music more appropriate for your age group."

"This is fine, Mom. I'm going to put the music on. Byron will be here soon."

Kimberly went back into the kitchen. As she checked the lemon chicken in the oven, she heard Luther Vandross's mellow voice filter into the room. Oh, God. What memories that song brought back.

The aroma of the chicken filled the air. She'd prepared Byron's favorite dish. Lemon chicken, garlic mashed potatoes and broccoli with asiago cheese. For desert she'd made a pineapple upside-down cake, which also happened to be Jack's favorite dessert. It held center stage at the table, on the crystal dessert plate.

Kimberly heard a car horn toot.

"That's Byron," April called out.

"I told that boy not to toot his horn, but to ring the doorbell," Kimberly scolded. "Where does he think he is?"

Kimberly heard the door slam on her words. She

peeped out the door and Byron's car shot off as soon as April got in. She was going to have to talk to him about his speed again.

Everything was fine in the kitchen, and Kimberly quickly went upstairs to change into black slacks and a sleeveless pink summer sweater she'd laid out earlier.

When she was passing the foyer she heard a key in the door. Puzzled, Kimberly moved forward. The kids couldn't be back this soon. Did April need money for the supplies?

Kimberly was surprised when Jack stepped through the door.

"What's wrong with the doorbell?" Kimberly asked. "You don't live here anymore."

"I'm still paying the mortgage."

"Which doesn't give you the right to frighten us half to death, walking in and out any time you please." Kimberly frowned. The beige linen slacks and brown shirt molding to his body took her breath away.

"I'm not going to fight with you over this, Kim. Where are the kids?"

"They went to the store. Why are you here?"

"April asked me to come. I'm supposed to meet Byron's new girlfriend."

"They didn't tell me you were coming."

"He's my son. I'm interested. Besides, April told me you knew."

"You may as well come in," Kimberly said ungraciously, then marched off to the kitchen.

"Well, thank you," Jack responded in a peeved manner. He followed her. "Do you need any help?"

"Everything is under control."

"Something smells good."

"Byron's favorite," she said.

Jack pulled out a barstool and sat. Damn, if Kimberly didn't look good with that sweater molding her breasts and the pants hugging her hips. They were a little tight. At least she was gaining weight. Did that mean she was getting over him? Already? Jack didn't like that.

A half hour came and went a half hour ago, and the kids still hadn't shown up. Kimberly worried they'd been in an accident. The food was ready to be dished into serving bowls and placed on the table.

She'd already dialed April's cell phone, and now she dialed Byron's. No answer from either of them. She dialed April again and left a threatening message. Less than a minute later, April called her.

"Where in the world are you?" Kimberly asked.

"Byron's girlfriend did something and she's being punished. She can't go out tonight."

"Why didn't you come home? Dinner is ready."

"Because Grandma called and we have to go over there to get something."

"Why didn't you call and tell me you were going to your grandmother's house?" Kimberly asked, knowing this was another one of April's schemes.

"I forgot how long it took."

"April…"

"Well, I did. We're almost at Grandma's. We can spend the night, can't we?"

"This is the last time you scheme to get your father and me together," Kimberly demanded, feeling like a heel for causing her children so much unhappiness. "Have your grandmother call me as soon as you get there. And the two of you are in big trouble," Kimberly said, annoyed. She might feel guilty, but she wasn't going to let them know. Now she was stuck alone with Jack, who would probably desert her, too.

"What's happening with the kids?" he asked, munching on the cake.

"Jack, what if the girl had come? You would have cut the cake?"

"I overheard the conversation. I've been salivating about that cake for the past hour. The smell is all through the house."

He looked so innocent, Kimberly laughed. "Would you like some dinner to go along with the cake?"

"That would be nice," he said.

Kimberly dished the food into bowls. The candles had burned down some, but the ambience was still romantic, which wasn't the mood she wanted to set with Jack.

"The candelabra and roses was April's doing."

"She fooled us, didn't she?"

"She did that," Kimberly said, setting the potatoes on the table. Jack held the seat for her as she sat. She couldn't remember the last time he'd made that gesture. Over the years, there were lots of little things they'd forgotten to do for each other.

They listened to Luther, the Temptations and Gerald LaVert while they ate the succulent dinner. Kimberly had to admit she'd outdone herself. And in the flickering candlelight, she couldn't help wishing Jack sat across from her each evening and that they'd go to bed together each night. He wore a golf shirt and linen slacks, and they looked absolutely great on him. She missed times like these.

"Ready for more cake?" she asked, more for something to do.

"Of course," he said, and she sliced him a thick piece and spooned two scoops of ice cream on top.

He rubbed his hands together as he waited for her to sit.

"Remember when Mom used to take the kids for Saturday night to give us a date night?" he asked.

"I remember," Kimberly said.

"I don't remember when we last had a date night."

Conversation lagged and they went back to their dessert, his words ringing in the air. When the last spoonful had been eaten, Larry Graham's "One in a Million" played, the soothing tune filling the room. It was their song, and sadness gathered in Kimberly's heart.

When she glanced up from her plate, Jack was beside her. "May I have this dance?" he asked.

Kimberly slowly rose and Jack gathered her into his arms. She closed her eyes with a sigh. It felt so good being molded against his body as they swayed to the mellow tones of the music. Kimberly pressed her face against his chest, feeling the steady rhythm of his heartbeat. He placed his arms around her and pulled her close.

Kimberly missed this. If she closed her eyes and listened intently she could forget all her problems and remember this was their song. Jack stroked her back, slid his hands down to her hips.

Kimberly's hands slid up his back, feeling the corded muscles beneath his skin. It all felt so familiar, so wonderful.

Jack's hand slid to her face, stroking her cheek with the back of his hand before he gathered her chin, tilted it and kissed her, first with small nibbling bites, then he entered her mouth fully with an all-consuming kiss.

Just one kiss, Kimberly thought, as she lost herself in the pleasure of the moment. She could taste the pineapple on his tongue. Their tongues dueled as if they couldn't get enough of each other. Having Jack in her arms was so familiar, so wonderful.

Jack caressed her nipples, pulling on the pebbled peaks, eliciting a deep moan from Kimberly's lips. She cried out in pleasure.

As the last note of the song ended, he gathered her in his arms and carried her upstairs to their room. He quickly undressed her and began to kiss her, then ran his tongue over her heated skin.

He stroked her thighs, her sensitive place, and Kimberly cried out in pleasure as he inched closer and closer to the heat of her desire.

He wrung a tumultuous orgasm from her before he entered her. Kimberly curled her legs around him and he sank deeper into her. He felt wonderful. Together, they moved in rhythm, until Kimberly cried out once again in pleasure. Jack's guttural moan followed closely behind hers.

They were lying spoon-fashion on the bed. Jack's arm was around her waist, rubbing her stomach. The other under her head. Kimberly tensed—until she realized she didn't show any signs of her pregnancy yet.

Jack kissed her neck, his breath brushed pleasantly over her skin. "Kimberly, as much as I would like to stay, I think I should leave. If the kids decide to come back, it would confuse them."

Kimberly nodded. It confused her. "We shouldn't have done this."

"You're still my wife."

"But we're separated. We can't do this again, Jack."

"We'll talk about it."

"There's nothing to discuss. You aren't sure of what you want. This was a huge mistake."

"All right. Have it your way. I don't understand why you're putting us through this, but I'll go along with it for now."

When Jack slipped out and stomped to the bathroom, Kimberly groaned. She felt sexually sated, but angry with herself. She should never have gone to bed with Jack, but she couldn't deny she'd needed him. God, she needed him like the air she breathed.

The next day, April was in the house before Kimberly made it out of bed. Kimberly was feeling tired lately, which was expected, given her pregnancy. Good thing she'd slipped into clothes after Jack had left.

"Where's Dad?" April asked.

"I don't know."

"He didn't spend the night?" April was clearly disappointed, and Kimberly wanted to wipe it from her face.

"No, honey. You know we're not together right now. We need to sort some things out."

"But I thought…"

"You thought you'd throw us together and everything would be okay?"

Kimberly got up and gathered her daughter into her arms. Byron stood at the door with a closed expression on his face. "Come on, Byron. Sit beside me."

Reluctantly, he came over and Kimberly threw an arm around his shoulder. He sat stiff in her embrace.

"Your father still loves you. He and I have to work a few things out. In the meantime, he'll be spending time with you and I'll spend time with you. But don't worry about us. We both love you very much. That hasn't changed."

"But we won't be together anymore. I thought our family would always be together."

"Honey, we'll work it out. Now, I'll fix French toast for breakfast and you get ready for church."

Friday night Jack worked late, more for something to do, rather than having to work. He just didn't feel like going to an empty apartment. He was accustomed to having noise around, to children running up and down the stairs—April yelling something at her mother as they got ready to go to a game, or practice or something.

It was funny, how he'd scold her about running, and now he missed those noises.

At least tomorrow night he had the poker game, but he'd already fielded calls from his family about the separation. He didn't feel like going through an in-depth explanation about that. How could he explain it to anyone else when he couldn't sort it out for himself?

He flipped the channel until he found a game. But before he really got into it, he nodded off.

A couple of hours later the phone rang. When the male voice announced that he was an officer with the police department, Jack straightened up, worried like heck about what had happened to someone in his family, but the officer told him Byron had been drinking beer and he had to pick him up.

Jack sped to the friend's house. The officer was still there, waiting for other parents to pick up their children. Jack spoke to the man before he ushered his son to the car.

He left Byron's car parked on the street. The boy reeked of beer as he drove to the condo Jack had sublet from a friend who was spending time in Europe.

He raked his son with a searing glance. "What the hell were you thinking, Byron?"

"It's just beer."

"You're sixteen. You know better. We've talked about you and alcohol. Were you planning on driving under the influence?" Jack's fingers cramped around the wheel. "Put lives in danger, not to mention your own? The privilege to drive also carries a great responsibility. Your car is a powerful machine, not a toy. I could ground you—take your license until you're eighteen. Do you want that?"

"I wasn't going to drive. I was going to spend the night there, remember? You gave me permission."

"I didn't give you permission to drink," Jack blasted. "Where are his parents?"

"They're out of town."

"Out of…" Jack gathered a breath to keep from backhanding his son. "You know the rules. You aren't allowed to stay overnight in a house without a responsible adult there. And what about this new girlfriend you were supposed to bring to the house? Why haven't your mother or I met her?"

"There isn't a girlfriend. April made it up to get you and Mom together."

"Byron…"

"I don't want to hear the lecture. I know I spoiled you getting your groove on with some hoochie mama."

"I wasn't out with another woman," Jack said between his gritted teeth. "I was home alone asleep. I'm still married to your mother. I wouldn't have an affair. What kind of man do you think I am? I've always tried to do the right thing. Tried to set a good example for you."

"Then why did you move out? If you want to do the right thing, why aren't you home with Mom?"

"Your mother and I have a few things to sort out."

"Whoever you have to sort out, I bet she's hot. I know the kind of women who hang out at those pubs."

"Most of them are hardworking women who just

want good food and someplace to socialize on the weekends and evenings. Or someplace to watch a game with friends or make new friends." Jack slanted a gaze to his son, who was slouched in the seat.

"You're not too young to start working, you know. School just ended. Maybe it's time you can train to be a waiter at one of the brewpubs. Give you a taste of the real world. At sixteen, I was holding down a job and going to school full-time."

"Yeah, I know. Grandma told me."

"My dad died when I was young. I work hard because I want you, your sister and your mother to be comfortable," Jack said. "I'm taking your driving privileges away for two weeks."

"Oh, Dad, come on. It's the summer."

"You broke the rules. Be ready to pay the consequences."

Byron slouched down in the seat even farther. "That's not fair."

"How do you think I felt when the cops called me? Can you imagine the nightmare running through my mind when he identified himself?"

"Some of the guys got a little loud."

"There were girls there, too. You're lucky they didn't take you all down to the station."

"You always exaggerate. I wasn't drag racing, or anything that bad."

"Every parent worries. And if I ever caught you drag racing you'd lose your car until you were fifty."

Jack caught the boy rolling his eyes.

"Better watch that."

"I'm not stupid. They had enough about it on the news. The news Mom makes me watch."

Jack smothered a smile. "You need to keep abreast of what's going on in your world."

The next day Kimberly met Jack for lunch, wondering why he wanted to meet with her when the children weren't around. They ended up at a restaurant close to their home.

He was dressed in his usual work attire. She'd changed into slacks and a red sweater top.

He stood when she reached the table, and kissed her on the cheek, which surprised her.

"How are you?" he asked.

"Fine."

Kimberly waited until the waitress took their order for drinks and dinner before she broached the reason they were there.

"Why this secret meeting?" she asked, taking a sip from her soda water.

"I got a call from the police last night. Byron was drinking at a party at his friend's house," Jack said.

"What happened?"

"The police called the parents to pick up their children. The parents weren't there."

"You didn't check before you let him go?"

"Do you always call the parents when he stays overnight?" Jack asked.

"Yes, I do. I know all his friends' parents."

"I guess I should have checked with you before letting him stay there."

"I'm going to give that boy a good talking-to. And punishment."

"I've already discussed it with him. And he's lost the use of his car."

"You don't think…"

"He assures me he wasn't going to drive after drinking, but I lectured him on that, too."

"Well, good."

"I'm going to let him work at one of the pubs this summer."

"That's a good idea. He shouldn't have so much free time on his hands. And he'll still be able to attend the summer programs that are scheduled." Kimberly sighed. "I tell you, you just don't know what they're going to do next. I'm so worried about him."

"Kimberly, all kids try drinking at his age. He's a boy."

"That's no excuse for breaking the rules."

"He's not a bad kid," Jack assured her.

"But he could—"

Jack touched her hand. "Honey, what he did was against the rules, but we'll keep talking to him. Believe it or not, they listen sometimes. I got out of line, too, now and then, but I turned out okay, didn't I?"

The way he was looking at her made Kimberly's heartbeat quicken. He turned out more than okay. "You turned out just fine, Jack."

"Well, at least we agree on something."

Kimberly smiled. "I don't think you're a bad person, Jack."

"I guess there's hope for me yet," he said, leaning back in his chair, looking sexy as heck.

It was the end of June, and Saturday night the Nationals, the local D.C. baseball team, was playing. Every channel on every TV situated around the brewpub was tuned in to it. As customers drank beer and wine, rowdy groups were yelling at the screens.

Byron was working out well as a waiter. He could serve food but not alcoholic beverages. Jack caught sight of the boy hurrying to a table with a tray of soft drinks.

Jack was sitting at the bar brooding, trying to decide if he was going to join his brothers and cousins for all-night poker. As he stared into his Pepsi, a leggy brunette sat on the stool beside him. She wore spiked heels, her skirt was short, and she was absolutely beautiful. It immediately kicked his mind back to when Kimberly had come into the bar wearing a black nothing, her legs looking fantastic in her spiked heels, her hair swaying along her smooth shoulders, and the fantastic lovemaking afterward.

It seemed like a lifetime ago.

Since she'd kicked him out, he had all the freedom in the world, but he still couldn't seem to come to terms with what started the argument.

He'd rented a three-bedroom condo. His new home didn't allow much space for the kids when they visited him on the weekends. April was still having a hard time adjusting to the new arrangement. Byron was more quiet, but Jack could tell the boy had issues over him moving out.

"May I get you a refill?" the woman asked. Jack had seen her around quite often lately. He hadn't had sex in a while with Kimberly. He was pissed off that she was putting them through this. What did she think she was going to do? She had to let him back.

Always something with women.

He glanced at the attractive sista beside him. He wouldn't have to work hard to get laid with her. And obviously, she was new and was unaware he was the owner.

"Why don't I buy *you* a drink?" he offered.

She nodded her thanks. "My name's Kasey."

"Pleasure to meet you, Kasey. I'm Jack." At one time he wouldn't have considered putting any effort into the chitchat. But now...if his wife didn't appreciate him, then someone else would.

"I think the Nationals have a good chance of winning tonight. Blake's doing very well," she said.

Jack shook his head. She could even keep the conversation going if he failed. "Yeah," Jack said, glancing at the screen. He hadn't been watching the game. But he watched her now.

"Do you watch baseball?" she asked.

"Of course," Jack said. Jack didn't even try to hide the ring glaring on his ring finger, but she didn't seem to mind.

"So, what are you doing by yourself tonight?"

"Just taking a break from work," he said.

"When do you get off?"

"Whenever I choose," he said.

The smile was sultry when she twisted in her chair, so that those long legs rubbed against his. He twisted in his bar stool, for a better view of Kasey.

"What about right now?" she asked.

He peered into her eyes, but all he saw was Kimberly's eyes. He glanced down at her legs and wanted to feel himself harden, but all he could remember were Kimberly's legs, damn it to hell. Because hell was exactly the place she'd sent him with her irrational behavior.

Kimberly had bewitched him from the moment he'd met her. And she still had some control over him. It was a curse. He wouldn't put it past those women to have worked up some roots, or some such curse to control him. Keep him in line. But he wasn't helpless. Jack's smile turned benevolent. He had a plan of his own.

He was a businessman. He'd never used wiles on his wife. He'd always been true to her. Always been up-front about his feelings and actions. But maybe it was time for him to put on a show to save his marriage. Wouldn't it be worth it? It was for her own good.

"Is that a yes?" the woman asked.

Shaking his head regretfully, Jack rubbed the ring on his finger.

"I thank you for the invitation," he said smoothly. "But I have to get back to work." Jack slid out of the seat. "Your drink's on me." At the other end of the bar, he signaled the bartender that he was picking up the lady's tab, then left.

His decision was made. He was playing poker. Byron wouldn't appreciate him spying on him anyway. He glanced at his son one last time before he left the bar. He had not expected his son to be watching him—glaring at him. For a little while, Jack had forgotten his son was even there.

The last thing he needed was for Byron to see him leaving the bar with another woman. Then all the negative thoughts the boy had about him would have been true.

Jack pushed his way through the swinging door a tad too forcefully. Fidelity was all fine and good, but it didn't help his sex-starved body one damn bit.

Once a month Jack had poker night with his brothers and cousins. Tonight they were meeting at his cousin Sam's place.

The men met in the pool house so that Sam's wife wouldn't complain about them getting cigar smoke in her curtains. This was Sam's man cave; the house was his wife's domain. Sam's wife hated cards. She was having some friends over, but they'd be in the house and wouldn't interfere with their game. Except the guys might go there for food later on.

"You all ready to lose? I'm feeling lucky tonight." Samuel had already lit his cigar.

It was pretty cool outside, so they opened windows before they settled down.

"So, what's going on with Kim and you? She let you move back in yet?"

"I got it all under control."

He heard a bark of laughter.

"You what?" Sam asked.

"Trust me." Jack frowned at the cards.

"Naw, man, don't even think that. It'll get you in trouble every time. Take some advice from an old head. Go back and apologize. Let her know she's right even if she's wrong."

"Better listen to him. He knows what he's talking about. When it comes to women, we never have it under control."

"You just wait and see," Jack said, assured in his ability to gain control over the situation. Damn it, he wore the pants in his house. No woman was going to put him out and watch him come back begging. She was going to beg him to come back.

Chapter 8

Kimberly was contemplating what she would do that Saturday evening, when her sister-in-law called.

"Girl, you had better get over here," Janice whispered in a furtive manner.

"I'm beat. I thought I'd watch a movie and go to bed early."

"You need to change your plans, girlfriend. Heard you were back on that part-time schedule," Janice said. "You had most of the week to rest. You need to come on over here."

"What's going on?"

"Wait a minute." Kimberly heard Janice saying something in the background but couldn't make out the words. Then she came back to the phone.

"Girl, the guys are playing poker in the pool house and…well. You and Jack are still separated, aren't you? I just wanted to make sure."

"Well, it's a tempo—"

"If I were you, I'd come over," Janice said, interrupting.

Her curiosity piqued, Kimberly said, "What's going on?"

"All the ladies are here and then some. Know what I mean? Everybody brought something to eat. I know it's last-minute for you, so don't worry about bringing a dish. We have more than enough. Just come."

"Janice—Janice—"

"We're going to have a party of our own," Janice said in a loud voice. "We have enough food for an army. Just playing music and chatting. We miss you, girl. You've made yourself scarce lately."

"Janice, what is going on?"

"Gotta go."

"Janice—"

Her sister-in-law hung up. Frowning, Kimberly slowly lowered her phone. What on earth was going on over there? It had to be Jack. Just what was he up to now?

There was no way Kimberly could *not* go. Nearly flying up the stairs, she had to stop and sit on the top step. Her stomach started roiling. She dashed to the bathroom just in time to throw up. The any-time-of-day morning sickness had come down on her hard.

She washed out her mouth and brushed her teeth. She was having his baby. He had no business with another woman. Illogically, she refused to acknowledge that he wasn't at home because she put him out.

She scanned the clothes in her closet, considering what to wear. Morning sickness came and went. She wasn't going to let it stop her from discovering what Jack was up to. She decided to go casual chic. She might not know the state of her marriage, but she wasn't going to let herself go. She chose white jeans with an aqua, sleeveless sweater, a gold necklace, earrings and bracelet.

She twisted the rings on her finger. Jack had bought her the four-carat diamond for their tenth anniversary. He'd opened three brewpubs by then.

Worry settled in Kimberly's chest and wouldn't let up. She didn't want to send Jack into the arms of another woman. *Have I waited too long?* Kimberly wondered when she started the car's engine. Could they repair something that was that broken? She'd reached the point where, outside of sex, she was living with a stranger—and Jack just didn't seem to care.

Most important, had Jack moved on? Was that the gist of Janice's call?

When Kimberly got there, the ladies were sitting around talking. Kimberly looked for an unfamiliar face, but she knew everyone there. They were either wives or dates.

"Kim," Janice said, approaching her, all innocence. "I'm so glad you could join us. We've missed you this summer, girl," she ran on without catching a breath. "Mom called the other day. She said she was going to the island with the kids this time," Janice said.

"They're looking forward to it." Kimberly still didn't understand why Janice had insisted she come. "I threw together a bean and pasta salad to contribute. Janice, why don't you come to the dining room with me?"

"Sure. I'll help make room on the table."

Kimberly waited until they were far enough away to talk without being overheard. "What's going on?" she hissed.

"Nothing. Who said anything was wrong?"

Kimberly gave her a level look. "Is Jack here with another woman?"

"No."

"Then why did you insist I come? And why did you have me believe he was?"

"I said no such thing. It's just…everyone missed you. Just like I said."

"Girl, don't play games with me. Now I know where April got her scheming from. You."

"Girl, you know Jack has more sense than to bring another woman here. We'd be all over him," she said. "And I'm not a schemer. I take exception to that."

"Oh, please. I could be getting some much-needed sleep, and here you're playing games." The dread in her chest had built to monumental proportions by the time she arrived. Now it slowly eased. She could strangle Janice for making her worry like that.

Janice hugged her. "You and Jack have been together way too long to split now. I have faith that you can fix this."

"I don't know," Kimberly said, feeling tiredness

stealing over her. She'd thought she and Jack would have been able to come to some equitable understanding long before now. But he was living his separate life and she was living hers—as usual. She didn't know if there was a solution. And she couldn't offer hope she didn't feel.

Since the women refused to bring food out to the pool house, the guys were forced to go to the house. The last person Jack expected to see was Kimberly.

The women were playing music and dancing. He searched Kimberly's eyes. She'd been laughing when he first came in, but now the laughter stopped. As a unit, the women glared at him as if the separation was all his fault.

He'd just like to have a chance to think and make a decision without their input. Since his family found out, he hadn't had a moment's peace. Everyone was giving opinions.

Sam went to his wife, hugged her. "Are you going to fix my plate, honey?"

She kissed him back just as sweetly. "Honey, I cooked. You can choose whatever you want, to your heart's desire, but first I want to dance," she said, tugging him into her arms. "Grab your husbands, ladies. Let's put on a slow one."

Sam groaned. "The trials of a married man. Maybe Kim will take pity on you, Jack, and fix your plate," he said, tugging his wife close. "Baby, you did put the arsenic away, didn't you?"

"Very funny, Sam," Kimberly said.

Kimberly's smile was as strained as Jack's. The other men sought out their wives, leaving Jack with no option but to gather Kimberly in his arms. She went along with it, but was as stiff as a board.

He couldn't help but wonder why she agreed to come. Did she really want to hear everyone's opinion about the separation? She knew they had to regale her as much as they did him.

Memories of the last time they made love floated back as Jack held Kimberly in his arms. She was warm and soft against him. At first, he thought to hold her away, but it seemed of his own volition that he soon tugged her closer. The rhythm of the music, the low lights, all seemed to conspire against his brain and focus on his body's needs.

"You feel different," Jack said, frowning.

"I haven't been exercising as much as usual."

"That must be it."

At first, Kimberly's movements were stiff; then she softened and danced as if all the drama of late hadn't transpired.

It was times like these that Jack didn't understand why they were going through this mess. He thought all would be better, once he moved out and began to do the things he'd always dreamed of, the things that a family and early marriage had cheated him of. But now that he had that freedom, the loss of family seemed too harsh a burden. He felt so guilty that he couldn't move past what he was doing to his wife and kids.

"I'm sorry, Kim."

"About what?"

"I feel guilty about leaving you and the kids."

"You feel guilty?"

"Yeah. Maybe I should come back. The kids are taking this pretty hard."

"Jack, I don't want you back for that reason. We'll be fine. I don't want you back unless I'm the one you truly want to be with. Not out of a sense of guilt or responsibility. The children will be fine. I'll be fine."

"Kim—"

"Jack, I've always felt that I had to put out more, do more to make you happy, to make the children happy, to make sure our marriage survived. I've always felt responsible for you having to marry me, but it wasn't just me. When I got pregnant at eighteen, you were as at fault as I was, and I don't feel responsible any longer. I'm not bending over backward to please you. I have some needs, too. I'm glad now that I'll be working part-time, because I do need to spend more time with the children. But I'm going to have some say in what goes on in my home."

He looked surprised. "You've always had a say."

"I've held back and let you take the lead."

"So, are you saying everything that went wrong in our marriage was my fault?"

"No, it's my fault for letting it disintegrate to this point. But, Jack, I'm not going to sit around moping while you find yourself. I'm going to live my life, even if I have to do it without you."

"You've been doing just great without me so far, haven't you? Are you seeing someone?"

"No. This has nothing to do with another man."

He studied her in silence before he spoke again. "It's not just you and me, Kim. April is having a difficult time with the breakup. And so is Byron."

"It will be painful for them in the beginning, but they'll adjust, especially if they know you'll still be a part of their lives. I think it's even more important now than before." Kimberly paused. "They'll be fine, Jack. Really. Like I said, I don't want you back for the kids. They're older. As long as you play an active role in their lives, they'll survive," Kimberly said. "You're free to explore your wildest dreams, whatever goals you haven't been able to achieve because I stood in your way. You're free. And, Jack, we're not going to be friends with benefits."

The thought that Kimberly might not be there when he got himself together had never crossed Jack's mind. He pictured her waiting for him while he tried to do that.

"I had dreams and goals, too. Your life wasn't the only one affected back when I got pregnant."

"So, is the guy you were with the other night the beginning of a new you?"

"That's none of your business."

"If he's around my kids, it damn well is."

"He's my new producer at the station," Kimberly said. "Remember, I told you about him?"

"Hey, you two. I thought you were supposed to be enjoying this mellow music," Sam said. "Looks like it's getting heavy over there." The music had stopped and Jack hadn't even realized it.

Ungrateful, he thought. He'd sacrificed his life so that his children could be born in wedlock, and his wife was ungrateful. How many millions of men wouldn't care less if the woman wasn't married when the child was born? But he'd done the right thing and she didn't even appreciate it.

"I need a cold drink," Jack said, and left for the buffet, but instead of pouring a shot of whiskey, he poured a glass of water. He might have to pick up April, and Kimberly was just ornery enough not to get the child, even knowing that he was in the middle of an important game. She'd been adamant about him seeing the children on weekends. Before the split, she'd mention it now and then, but now she'd become downright hostile about it. What had happened to the nice, malleable woman he was married to? She'd changed into a totally different person.

He took a long swallow of water, when his mother and kids walked in. Jack sighed heavily. All he needed was another lecture from her. He should have gone to his lonely apartment.

Kimberly dashed to the bathroom. Frowning, his mother followed her. When they were still back there after five minutes, Jack knew they were talking about him. His mother—his entire family—adored Kimberly. According to them, the separation was entirely his fault, even though he wouldn't discuss it with them. He knew Kimberly wouldn't.

Jack finally gave up waiting for Kimberly and began fixing his plate. When they finally returned, his mother was all smiles until she leveled her gaze on him. What had he done now, other than the obvious?

"Why didn't you tell me Kimberly was pregnant?" she asked.

"She's…" Jack glared at Kimberly. That was it.

She'd lied to him. He'd asked her on Canter Island and she actually lied. He couldn't believe she'd lie to him about something so important.

"Jack, Kim always had bad morning sickness, and it happens any time of the day," his mother said. "Don't you remember?"

"I haven't told him yet," Kimberly murmured.

"Lord, Lord, Lord. Another little one. Aren't we blessed?" His mother sighed, sending a searing glance to her other children before her gaze settled on Jack again. "Seems you're the only one who's ever going to give me grandchildren, but I welcome every one of them."

But Jack wasn't listening to his mother's raving. He grabbed Kimberly's hand and tugged her outside.

"Why did you lie to me?" Jack demanded.

"I didn't lie to you. I wasn't pregnant when you asked me."

"When *did* you get pregnant?"

"Probably the day of the hurricane, or at least when we were on vacation."

"You knew all this time, yet never mentioned it once. *Not once.* You knew I would have come back."

"Exactly the reason I *didn't* tell you. I don't want you back for that reason."

"If you think a child of mine is going to be born—"

"It's not just your child. It's mine, too, and I have some say in this," Kimberly rebutted.

"You've had too much to say lately. You're not keeping me out of my own house."

"Then I'll move out."

Jack's whole being was stamped with frustration. "Now I understand why you've been irrational lately."

"I'm not irrational. If you want to ignore everything that's happened, and label it under the heading of 'crazy wife,'" she said, making little quote marks with her index fingers, "be my guest. It's not going to get you back in that house with me."

Kimberly left him outside and stormed into the house. She was hungry. Jack could damn well do what he wanted.

Kimberly couldn't believe the words that had poured from her. Yet she was glad she'd said them. She believed every one of them. She valued herself too much to play second fiddle, or hold on to a man who didn't really want her. She still loved Jack, but she wasn't willing to destroy herself for that love.

Jack's sister linked her arm through Kimberly's. "The guys are going to grab food and take it to the pool house. We're going to chow down, too. Oh, Kim." Janice's eyes filled with tears and so did Kimberly's. "I'm so happy for you. You've wanted another child for so long." She grabbed Kimberly in a bear hug, nearly crushing her.

Kimberly blinked the tears back.

From across the room, Jack watched the exchange between Kimberly and his sister. Kimberly looked radiant. Her breasts were fuller. Her skin glowed with health. Absolutely beautiful. Jack felt his heart clench at the unexpected pleasure and frustration. Desire, hot and immediate, spread through him like molten lava.

His sister finally let go of Kimberly from the bear hug and someone else took her in her arms. They were making their rounds. Suddenly, her eyes touched his. He knew she saw the desire he didn't even try to hide. And something delicious and hot flickered in her eyes. She wasn't immune to him, not by a long shot. She might give him grief, but on one level they were always on the same page.

They were having another baby. At thirty-eight, some men would want to put child rearing behind them, but he loved his children.

His eyes caressed Kimberly as if he were touching her. She was still watching him, and he saw the blush steal over her features. She wiped her brow. How could he have missed the signs? He wanted to lift Kimberly into his arms and walk off with her, like a caveman. He wanted to take her to bed and make love through the night.

But he could imagine just what Kimberly was thinking—that this time, like twice before, he'd leave her to raise the child alone.

Things were different now. Both of them were older. Jack frowned. He'd participate more. He wouldn't give her room to complain.

Sam patted him on the back, tearing him from his thoughts. They did a high five.

"Congratulations, man. We've got to pull out the Cuban cigars for you. It's a day to celebrate."

Jack swiped a hand across his head. With the way his world had turned upside down, he was a long way from celebrating. But he knew one thing. He *was* moving back home. Kimberly wasn't in a rational frame of mind.

She needed him.

Jack signed the final papers for the bar in Prince George's County earlier that day. Any business deal he'd ever negotiated had gone better than negotiations with his wife.

"Hey, hey," Lauren said, handing a tall glass of beer to him. "Congratulations."

The glasses clinked and Jack took a long swallow. It went down smoothly, but the victory was bittersweet. In the past, the celebrations had always included Kimberly. This was the first time he was celebrating without her. And he was saddened and frustrated.

They should be celebrating the baby he wanted so badly, too. Was she happy about the pregnancy? Did she think this child was going to get in the way of her career? Was that the reason she kept it a secret? And had she known she was pregnant when he'd asked her on Canter Island? She'd said no. Could he believe her?

God. Now he was questioning her integrity.

His staff members approached to shake his hand.

With the openings of the last two bars, though, Kimberly had seemed less enthusiastic. He should have noticed the signs.

But suddenly he wanted to be with her. They were still married. This was as much her success as it was his.

"I have to leave. I'll see you tomorrow," he said.

It was the height of rush hour, and the drive to his house took forty-five minutes.

He missed driving in the neighborhood. Waiting to see the children going about their business, Kimberly rushing around the house with one task or another. Or asleep, if he came in late. Mundane, everyday things, but he missed them. He would not miss this baby growing up.

He debated whether he should use the key or ring the doorbell. Any little thing set her off. This time he parked in the driveway, not in the garage. He wondered if his spot was still empty.

This was still his home. He wasn't ringing any doorbell. He took out his key and opened the front door, but before he stepped completely in he called out Kimberly's name.

"Kim," he shouted. But she didn't respond. "Kim," he called again. When the house remained quiet, he went to the garage. Her car was there. Closing the door, he headed to the stairs and to their bedroom.

Kimberly was sleeping soundly on the bed.

He smiled. Expectant mothers needed their rest. He was having another baby. Jack couldn't help the deep warmth that spread through him.

Jack started to wake her, but instead he shucked his shoes and laid on the bed beside her, pulling her into his arms. He rubbed his hand over her abdomen. There was a small bulge. He'd thought it was from weight gain. Kimberly felt warm and soft in his embrace. She moved closer to him and he snuggled her tightly against him. This was how it should be.

Holding her in his arms and dancing during the poker game had been pure torture. He wanted to strip off her clothes and kiss her all over, touch her until she screamed for mercy. But he didn't.

He didn't want her to hold one more thing against him.

He breathed in deeply, inhaling the sweetness that was always a part of her. He missed this most of all, he thought, as, for the first time since Canter Island, he drifted off to sleep in the middle of the day.

Kimberly came awake slowly and smiled. Eyes still closed she rubbed her hand up the arm thrown across her waist. She felt warm and contented. Her eyes opened slowly.

And then she started, and twisted sharply, barely holding in a yelp. She swallowed hard to keep her stomach from roiling.

"What are you doing here?" She pressed a hand to her chest. She hadn't slept well since Jack left.

Jack's eyes popped open. "Umm." He rolled over in bed.

Kimberly scooted toward the center of the bed. "You didn't answer my question."

"I came to talk to you, but you were asleep. I thought to rest a few minutes, but I must have dozed off, too."

"What was I doing plastered up against you?" Kimberly asked suspiciously.

"I was asleep, baby. How would I know?"

She continued to give him a skeptical look, but Jack wouldn't change his story.

"Why did you come by?"

"I'd like all of us to go out to dinner."

He was upping his war to move back in—for the baby's sake.

"Why?"

"Why not? This separation is tearing the family apart. We need to do something together."

Kimberly resisted the urge to tell him she'd been saying that for years and he hadn't listened.

"Why don't you take the children to dinner?"

"Why can't you come?"

Kimberly shook her head. "I don't know if it's a good idea."

"Can't we eat together? Do you have to make everything so difficult, Kim?"

"Fine." Kimberly got up to go to the bathroom to brush her teeth and dress.

When the kids got home, April was ecstatic to see her father.

Byron was overjoyed, too, although he wasn't as effusive with it as April was. They drove to a restaurant close by.

Both of the children were happy about the new baby.

As they walked to the door, April pulled her father aside. "Are you moving back home?"

"Not yet."

"Oh."

"Chin up."

They were led to tables and studied menus, then ordered drinks and dinner. The waiter brought filled glasses to the table.

"I forgot to congratulate you on the new brewpub, Dad," Byron said.

Kimberly's gaze swiveled to Jack. "New brew-pub?" she asked.

"I signed the papers today," he said. "You know, the place I always wanted finally came on the market and I was able to buy it."

She held up her glass of iced tea. "Congratulations." But something died inside her. She guessed this was their last hurrah.

Jack knew exactly what Kimberly was thinking. And it was all wrong. He'd been thinking a lot since Lauren's comment about him being too hands-on, and had begun to give his managers more control in the pubs. He'd been sticking closer to the main office lately, surprising everyone.

"So, how do you like your new job, son?"

"It's okay."

"How would both of you like to be more involved in the process of renovating the new pub? You'd get to see what happens after a property is purchased. Everything from the architectural plans, the interior designer, staffing and the big grand opening."

"Really, Dad?" April asked.

"I think it's time."

"What about Mama?"

"She can, too, if she wants to."

April's eyes lit on Kimberly.

Smart move, Jack thought. If she didn't come aboard, she'd look churlish.

"We'll see," Kimberly said. The last thing she

wanted to talk about was brewpubs. It was Jack's obsession with them that was damaging their marriage. Although she wanted her children to have solid work ethics, she hoped he wasn't teaching the children to be workaholics like he was.

"The kids have school, but they'll have time."

"It's summer now, and we'll do a lot before school even starts," Jack said. "Can't afford to have an empty building."

"Can we go by there tonight?" Byron asked.

"I don't see why not. You don't work tomorrow, do you, Kimberly?"

"No," she said quietly.

"Then we'll go after dinner." Jack really wanted Kimberly to be happy about this project.

After Lauren's comment, he realized he was keeping part of his life from Kimberly. It was divided in different segments. His work, his children and his wife. But maybe he should show more interest in her work, maybe even help with her volunteer work. And bring her onboard with his projects so she'd feel more included.

He gazed at Kimberly. "Shall we celebrate with a glass of wine? What will you have?"

"Lemonade," she said. Convincing her wasn't going to be easy. Jack ordered a glass of chardonnay, and when he made the toast, her lemonade glass touched his wineglass. He knew he couldn't hang a lot of hope on that one move, because she could very well be putting on an act for the children. But for the first time that day, he felt hope build in his chest.

After dinner, he drove them to the new site. His lawyer had handed him the key just that day, and he pulled it out to open the door. There was an air of desertion about the place, although the old furniture was still in place. The parking lot was empty. No music filtered from the door.

"They're going to haul all the furniture out in a couple of weeks," Jack said.

"I want to watch, Daddy," April said.

"Of course you can. We'll all watch. I'll schedule it for when you're off, Kim."

She nodded.

"We own both of these units. The walls are going to be knocked out, and we'll have one room large enough to encompass both the restaurant and bar."

"Is it going to look like the other bars?" Byron asked.

"Exactly like the others."

"This doesn't look anything like your bars, Dad."

"It will. See those condos going up over there? This place is within walking distance of single-family homes, town houses and condos. A great customer base. People don't cook as much as they used to. Everyone's busy."

"Most of my friends' moms don't cook much, but Mom's a great cook," April said loyally.

"Yes, she is," Jack agreed. Even some of his cousins' wives rarely cooked. Often, they stopped by his place for takeout. Funny, he hadn't thought about it until April mentioned it. Even when Kimberly was busy, she prepared nutritious meals for the family.

"Did I ever tell you how much I appreciated that?" Jack asked.

Kimberly threw him a surprised look. "No."

"Well, I do." He tapped April on the nose. "And you two should appreciate the fact that you don't have to eat cold cereal or energy bars in the mornings. Your mama has me fixing oatmeal from scratch, hot pancakes and real eggs. You get a real breakfast. That's your mother's plan, also," he said. "Not mine."

"You actually prepare the meals," Kimberly said. "That's a big deal."

"I followed your schedule." Jack smiled. "We're becoming each other's cheering committee."

April beamed and Byron looked on in approval.

Kimberly couldn't help but wonder if this was one of Jack's games to enlist the children against her if she didn't come in line with his plan.

"I realize that, in the past, I haven't talked much about what I do. But it's important that you become a part of this business," Jack said to the kids. "It's all going to be yours one day."

As disappointed as Kimberly was about Jack's new purchase, she didn't know how to read this change in attitude. She didn't know whether it was a change or just an act. But bringing them all out there for once was different. Letting the children participate was different, too. She couldn't deny the kids were thrilled about being included.

It was dusk, and Jack was pointing out some things to the children. They were soaking it all in like sponges. All this would be theirs one day. It stood to reason that they should be involved in the business. They weren't too young to appreciate it.

"How do you like your new job, Byron?" Kimberly asked during a lull.

"I love it. I can even serve by myself now."

"Boy was a quick learner," Jack said.

"I want to work, too, Daddy," April said.

"I'll find something for you to do. You're a little young yet to work in the restaurant, but we can find something for you in the office."

The kids went off to peep into the building.

"Nice going, Jack. I hope you don't disappoint them."

"The way I've disappointed you?" he said, peeved that all his efforts were taken the wrong way.

"You're making an effort now, but will it continue when you're in the thick of your new project? Was all this to lure me into believing you've changed?"

The anger seemed to drain from Jack. "Kim, Kim," he said, shaking his head. He moved behind her, wrapped his arms around her, his hands moving tenderly over her womb. "You've got to learn to trust me, baby." He planted a sweet kiss just beneath her earlobe, hearing her quickly indrawn breath.

Jack moved his hands higher. Her heartbeat had definitely increased.

He wanted to buy her a gift, but she'd put the wrong interpretation on it, accuse him of getting it for the baby, and not for her.

Either way, he'd come up on the wrong side of her temper. What was a man to do?

Chapter 9

Kimberly kept thinking of her mother. She didn't want to end up losing her husband because they were living parallel lives—both headed down a narrow road, but not together. Nor did she want to raise this child alone. But Jack was happy about her pregnancy and was ready to do the chivalrous thing. In the past month, Jack had spent more time with her and the kids than he'd done in the previous six months. She was close to giving in.

It was the beginning of August, and the children were spending a couple of weeks with Jack's brother in the Caribbean. Kimberly had thought it was the perfect time for them to talk and sort out some things. But now, all of her old worries were creeping back in, and she wasn't so sure. She'd never been away from Jack so long.

Truthfully, Kimberly missed the children terribly. Three days with them gone gave her the feel of how things would be when they left for college.

The house was lonely without the extra noise and fights. Of course, this little one would definitely keep her busy. And as tired as she got of them fighting, she'd rather endure that than this aloneness. But they enjoyed their trips to the island. And besides, she had her friend's wedding coming up. Her sorority sister from college was getting married, so she could forget her problems and share in someone else's joy. The wedding party was arriving soon, and at least she'd be busy with friends and sorority sisters.

Kimberly wasn't in a celebratory mood tonight, but she'd hired the woman who usually did her cleaning to spend the weekend, because three of her sorority sisters were staying with her.

Since most of her friends from school were scattered all over the country, the bridal shower was to be held at Kimberly's house the next night. She'd had the cleaning crew in that week. The wedding rehearsal was Friday, followed by the rehearsal dinner.

The bachelor party was tomorrow night, too, at one of Jack's brewpubs. No doubt they'd have women there for a great send-off.

Kimberly thought the shower would depress her, but she found herself having a wonderful time, socializing with her old friends.

She still didn't know what to feel about Jack's new behavior. Maybe she should give him the benefit of the doubt.

They'd already played Bride Bingo, word games and a couple of adult games, with prizes ranging from the sedate to the slightly kinky. They listened to music and danced.

And when the bride-to-be opened the gift from Vicky, there were two gifts inside, one for Kimberly, as well as one for the bride.

"What's this?" Kimberly asked, tearing off the wrapping paper.

"I thought the two of you could benefit from this one," Vicky said, with a smug smile on her face. The book was entitled, *How to Make Your Man Behave in 21 Days or Less, Using the Secrets of Professional Dog Trainers.*

"No, you didn't," Kimberly said.

Vicky shrugged. "Thought you could use a few pointers. And since we have a new bride here, she needs advice on getting it right."

Someone took the book out of Kimberly's hand and flipped through the pages.

"I like this one about flight and chase."

"Oooh. I like that," someone said. "Especially when he catches me."

"*He's* doing the flight, honey. This tells you how to *catch* him."

Kimberly hadn't laughed so much in ages.

But the bride's mother hustled the bride off before midnight. Dress rehearsal was tomorrow.

Kimberly didn't believe for a moment that the guys would retire before the next morning.

She sighed. She had guests to entertain, so she went upstairs to the top floor to shoot the breeze with them.

It was like a pajama party of old, when they would sit up until the wee hours of the morning, talking about nothing and everything.

"Hey, Kim," one of her sorority sisters said, "my husband and I stayed at Canter Resort last winter. It was some trip. And Jack's brother is handsome. I tried to hook him up with my sister, but he came up with some lame excuse. Do you think you can help me out?"

"I wish I could."

"I'm sorry about Jack and you. I fell in love with him myself when we were in college. I didn't think anything could come between the two of you."

Kimberly sighed, thinking of their first year together.

"You all were inseparable," the friend added.

Kimberly hadn't really discussed this with anyone but her makeup guy at the station. He talked a lot, but they kept each other's confidences. He'd told her to let Jack come back and get over herself. Jack was too hot to leave on his own for too long. According to him, her problem was all hormones, anyway.

The guy might be gay, but he was male, and of course he didn't understand.

"Kim, I saw you on the news when the storm came through. Girl, you looked like the wind was going to just whisk you away. Isn't that dangerous?"

"Doesn't Jack mind?" someone else asked.

"I take safety precautions. Besides, it was only a category one. I didn't sensationalize it. It's the drama that frightens people. I'm not going to stand out there if the wind is strong enough to blow me away, or for me to get hit by flying debris." She wasn't about to respond that Jack had hit the roof when she told him she had to go out for a news bite in the middle of the storm.

"Kimberly, we have career day each fall. Can I contact you about giving a talk?" one of her sorority sisters asked. "I think the children will find it exciting."

"I'll be happy to, if I'm free," she responded. "Just give me a call," she said.

They talked for an hour before she went to her bedroom, showered and dressed for bed.

But when she got under the covers that night, she couldn't get Jack off her mind. Had she made the wrong move in letting him go? The truth was, she never expected a divorce. She just wanted to shake Jack up to get him to consider some of her needs.

Kimberly didn't know what to think. It was one thing to trust, but another to be a complete, trusting fool.

Darn it, she missed Jack. When the kids were here he had an excuse to come by. With them gone, although he called daily to make sure she was okay, his visits had stopped.

She tossed and turned to get into a comfortable position, but couldn't. Earlier that week, she'd sprayed a light film of Jack's cologne on the pillow, just to smell his scent. Finally, she hugged his pillow in her arms. It seemed to calm her a little, but it wasn't like having the man.

The bachelor party was held in one of the empty banquet rooms at Jack's newest brewpub. The music was loud, and someone had even sprung for a woman to pop out of a "cake." Jack sat nursing a single beer.

One of his college friends would definitely be taking a cab home, Jack thought, as the man started on another bourbon.

"I understand you and the wife have split," Russ said.

"We've got some things to work out. But that's it," Jack said, still peeved that Kimberly distrusted him. He wasn't about to go into details about his wife with anybody. How the heck did this guy find out?

"Tell her she better treat you right," he said in a slurred voice, "because the women are coming after us. All kinds. Black, white, Hispanic, Asian. Man, the field is wide-open."

"Kim can say the same thing. She's a fantastic woman."

"You operate a bar, man. Get your nose out of your corporate office and take a look around. All kinds of single women are looking for men these days. We don't have to settle."

"I don't consider myself settling. But that's a two-way street. Kim doesn't have to settle either. Man, is that all a sister is to you? What about respect? What about all the times they had our backs? Is this the way we pay them back?"

"You're the one who walked out. At least, that's what I heard."

Jack moved away before he hit the guy. You couldn't reason with a drunk. If a knucklehead approached his daughter with that attitude, he hoped she'd send the guy to him, because he'd quickly reeducate him. And Kimberly. She had too much going for her to be thought of that way.

Kimberly was feeling a little queasy. She got up to drink a ginger ale. When she got to the fridge, she thought she heard a noise. More than likely, it was just the house settling, but still, fear crept up her spine. She grabbed a huge candlestick and flicked off the light.

She'd told Jack a thousand times they needed a secure lock on the door that led into the garage, but he assured her the outside door was secure. First thing after work Monday, she was calling a locksmith. She should have done it before.

When she got to the hallway, a light popped on. Kimberly froze in place. She should have dialed 911. But she'd thought it was her imagination. Oh, Lord. The footsteps were coming in her direction. What on earth? She hefted the candlestick above her head.

The man stepped through the door. She brought the candlestick down. He saw her at the last minute and jumped aside so that it landed on his shoulder, instead of his head.

"Damn it!" Jack shouted. "What is it with you? Are you trying to kill me or something?"

"Jack?" Kimberly said.

"Who else do you think it would be?"

"I thought it was a break-in."

"In this neighborhood?"

With shaky hands, she set the candlestick on the table. "This neighborhood doesn't have a fence around it."

"I just came by to pick up my tux."

"I told you to ring the doorbell when you came, not to just walk in."

"I thought you were asleep. Didn't want to wake you."

"You can't just walk into the home of a single woman, especially when she isn't expecting you."

He glared at her. "You're not a single woman, and last time I looked it's still my home, too."

"You moved out."

"You *put* me out."

"You wanted to be a free man. Besides, you were supposed to be at the bachelor party, chasing women. How was I to know you were coming to my house?" she said sarcastically.

"I wasn't chasing women, damn it. My shoulder hurts like hell." He glared at her.

"You should have called first," Kimberly repeated, strolling to the kitchen to put crushed ice in a freezer bag. "Do you want a painkiller?"

"It would help."

"Don't be such a baby," Kimberly said, handing him the ice bag. She got aspirin from the cabinet and a bottle of water from the fridge, handing them both to him.

Jack sat on a bar stool and Kimberly sat beside him. He wore his signature scent. She just wanted to be near him, even though he was mad as heck.

"I'm out of the house for a couple of months, and everything goes to hell."

"I'm doing just fine, thank you very much," Kimberly assured him.

"Yes, you are. You've turned into a new woman. Byron's acting crazy. April's a basket case. And you've become the Wonder Woman of the block."

"It's good to know I can protect myself."

Jack grumbled. "I came back to see how you were holding up. And to see if you are ready to be reasonable."

"Reasonable?"

"About everything. I don't know why you think I don't want this marriage, or why you think Lauren and I are having an affair."

Kimberly didn't know what to say.

"Where're the women?" he asked.

"Our party didn't last as long as yours. They're upstairs sleeping."

He noticed her drinking the ginger ale. "Queasy stomach?"

She nodded.

"I guess all the stress has worn on you," Jack said. He put the ice bag on the countertop.

"Guess so." She picked up the ice. "You need to keep the ice on your shoulder."

Slowly Jack slipped the ice back in place.

Kimberly didn't know how to read Jack's actions.

She didn't know why he was here. What happened tonight? Was he back because he didn't think she was capable of taking care of herself?

Jack sighed. "We need to talk, Kim."

"I know," she said.

"I was so grateful you worked with me in the beginning, when I wanted to buy the first brewpub. You paid the living expenses and let me save all of my money to put toward the pub. I wouldn't have been able to buy the first one so soon if you hadn't done that. So this isn't just my business, it's yours, too."

"You've never been selfish, Jack. You're a generous soul."

"I wanted to give you everything you ever wanted."

"But I wanted you."

"The boyfriend you left back home was wealthy," Jack said. "He could have given you everything."

"Is that why you've always worked so hard, why you can't seem to cut back, even though you've far surpassed my ex-boyfriend's wealth? He didn't create that wealth. It was handed to him." Kimberly cupped Jack's cheek in her hand. "Jack, I fell in love with *you*. It's true I wanted a comfortable living. But I never asked for the world."

"It isn't your way. But a man wants to live up to certain expectations. All I know is work. My old man worked hard. It's what I believe in. I never wanted to be a disappointment."

"You mean *your* expectations. You and I, along with your sisters and brothers, own an island resort. You have five successful brewpubs. This house…" She threw up her hands. "Financially, how could you be a disappointment?"

Jack put the ice pack down and reached across the table to grasp Kimberly's hand.

"I think I've been so busy trying to build a life around just-in-case, that I've forgotten about the life I have right now. There are the kids and keeping a business going. You know my dad worked really hard, almost as hard as I do. He saved for college for our futures, but four years later it was all gone. My stepfather destroyed everything it took my dad years to build. I wanted to make enough so that nothing like that happened to you and the children. I've been focusing on the wrong thing, and we got lost in the shuffle." He pulled her close. "I don't want to lose you, baby."

"I love you, Jack. I know how to handle money. I'd never let that happen to us. Besides, I work, too. So you aren't in this alone." Kimberly closed her eyes briefly. Did he believe this, or was he telling her what he thought she wanted to hear, because of the baby? That they'd have to start from scratch with this little one. She rubbed her hand across her stomach. Perhaps for once she should stop second-guessing and just believe him. He'd said all along he would have married her anyway. Perhaps it was time to let her insecurities go.

Jack tossed the ice on the bar and lifted her on his lap. "Stomach still upset?"

"Just a little."

"Want me to spend the night?"

Kimberly moaned, leaning her head against his neck. "That's not a good idea."

"I guess I should grab the tux and get back to the party, or everybody's going to have headaches—if they make it at all."

Kimberly nodded and slipped off his lap.

Testing his shoulder, Jack dumped the ice in the sink and made his way upstairs with Kimberly. It still hurt like hell, but the ice and pain medication took the edge off.

The truth was, he just had to see Kimberly tonight. There was this driving need to hold her. And there she sat, as calm as she pleased, in pajama shorts and a tank top.

He sucked in a breath, balled his hands into fists to keep from kissing her breathless.

In the bedroom, Jack stopped and breathed in deeply. It smelled feminine. Kimberly's perfume drifted lightly in the air. It wasn't cloying or heavy, but delicate. He was getting a hard-on just thinking about the scent on her warm skin.

Jack swiped a hand across his face. How many times had he come home at night and Kimberly's sweet aroma drifted softly in the air? It had brought calmness to a hectic day. He realized it had always done so. Now he was restless and edgy, unable to relax.

He'd been in the house for less than an hour, and already he'd calmed down. He was lonely without her.

"I have to go to Florida next week to a beer pairing and competition," Jack said at the reception after the wedding, as he and Kimberly danced to a slow, soulful song. God, it felt good holding her.

"You're competing more and more lately."

"Competitions get the name out. Hang a few certificates on the wall. Show a few ribbons."

"You've always been proud of the fact you serve great beer," she said.

"Yeah. Can't forget my roots," he said. "I guess I'm just getting to the point where I understand that you love your work, too," he said, pulling her closer. "I'm sorry I pressed you into cutting your hours. Especially now that someone is filling the slot and you can't go back."

"I'm glad I cut my hours."

He glanced at her skeptically. "Are you sure?"

"I wouldn't have changed them if I wasn't."

The band was playing "One in a Million." Jack pulled Kimberly tightly against him as the flow of the words washed over her.

"We'll have to talk this through once and for all," Jack said. "I've been holding a lot of things inside because I knew how you felt about the brewpubs. But I can't live like that anymore. So, when I get back from Florida, we'll sit and talk about our future."

Kimberly closed her eyes tightly and nodded against his chest.

"Okay, Kim?"

Kimberly cleared her throat.

"Yes," she said, and then the music stopped.

She left Jack's side to join the friendship circle, where the sorority sisters joined hands and sang their song.

Chapter 10

The next morning, Kimberly made plane reservations to leave for Canter Island after work Tuesday, and to return home on Sunday, giving her plenty of time to prepare for work Monday morning. She needed a few days to think. They were well into storm season, but there weren't any hurricanes looming close by. Not like the last time. Besides, if her children were there, she certainly could be with them.

Since the kids were with his brother, at the last minute Jack decided to call Kimberly to convince her to travel with him to Florida. This beer competition was really important, and he'd like to have her by his side. He'd always treated his work separate from her. He should have included her more. Let her be part of his world.

He called the house and received no answer. He dialed her cell number and still no answer, so he left a message. He tried to reach her for hours without success.

She must be avoiding him.

With a heavy heart, Jack boarded the plane for Tampa alone, his mind on his wife.

Although Kimberly was close to her children, she saw little of them on the island. She stayed in a cabana alone, while Jack's mother and the children resided at Devin's house. It gave her plenty of time to think and read. She was tired of trying to solve her problems.

She dug a snack out of her beach bag. She bit on a dry cracker and chased it down with ginger ale. It was near sunset, and she sat on the beach in her bathing suit to watch the waves come and go. What a beautiful view.

Maybe Jack loved her in the only way he knew. He could have left her any time, but he'd stuck around, even before he knew she was pregnant. He could have started up a relationship with another woman at any point this summer, but he chose to stick it out with her.

Sadly, there was no way for him to prove he would have married her if she hadn't been pregnant. She was just going to have to accept and live with that. It was certain she'd never find another man she loved as much as she loved Jack.

Ah, wasn't their wedding beautiful? She just wished

that thirty years in the future everything would be as perfect as that one day.

Perhaps she should count her blessings. Jack was good to her. Life wasn't perfect, but she could still wish for it to be better. She just wished she didn't feel so empty.

The afternoon before Jack was to board the plane for home, he called the children and reached Byron. He was told April had gone shopping on the main island with her grandmother. Jack chuckled. Those two loved to shop.

"How is it there?" he asked.

"Great. I went deep-sea fishing with Uncle Devin. I caught the biggest grouper, Dad. The chef is going to serve it as the night's special. Uncle Devin and I were up way before daybreak."

"Before daybreak? I need a siren to haul you out of the bed in the morning."

Byron laughed. Jack could detect a distinctive change in his voice. He was definitely growing up. "This was fun."

"I used to fish with my stepfather."

"I didn't know you knew how to fish."

"Sure I do. Where's your uncle?"

"He took Mama sailing. Said she was spending too much time moping around the hotel."

"Your mother's there?" Jack asked, surprised.

"She came yesterday. Didn't you know?"

"She must have forgotten to mention it," Jack said, indignant that she'd go without telling him.

"You can call her later, but I think Uncle Devin's taking her to dinner to eat my fish."

"Wish I could taste it. I bet it's some fish."

"The chef's freezing some for me to take home."

"That's good," Jack said.

Jack couldn't stop the jealousy that soared through him like a bolt of lightning. He couldn't get his mind off Devin sailing with Kimberly. Sailing was a special memory from their first honeymoon. She shouldn't be reminiscing with his brother.

He knew his brother would never do anything inappropriate with Kimberly, but...

Jack felt...*excluded.* Why was Kimberly in the Caribbean now, anyway? He thought she was home. She never went there when the kids visited his brother.

"Uncle Devin took the week off to spend with us," Byron was saying, which didn't ease Jack's anxiety at all.

Had Kimberly just quit talking and decided to live her life without him?

"Well, give my love to everyone. I'll see you, so..." Byron had already hung up. Deep in thought, Jack hung the phone up slowly.

He couldn't even consider visiting the island again. Things were just too busy at home. Kimberly knew that, even if she didn't like it. There were a million things to be done at the new property, to get it up and running in three months. Otherwise, it would be a financial drain during a time it should be producing. He couldn't afford to miss the holiday rush. A week ago he'd approved the advertising brochure. He was sending out packages to area businesses, letting them know the pub would be available to host holiday parties.

Jack shook his head. He couldn't get away to while away a few days on the island. He had to do the responsible thing.

He wanted the brewpub completely renovated in less than three months, in plenty of time for the holiday season. He'd open with holiday specials. His brewmaster was even developing a special beer for it.

When Jack first opened, he'd been the brewmaster for his pub. He liked that part of the business, but didn't have the time or opportunity to participate in that any longer.

Jack heard raised voices. He left the hallway and went back to the competition.

He'd call Kimberly from the hotel room tonight. At least they'd have some connection. She'd know he was thinking of her.

Devin helped Kimberly from the small sailboat.

"That was great."

"Jack should see you now. Your hair's all wind-blown. Your face is animated and healthy from the sea breeze. Call him, Kim. Ask him to join you here. He loves you."

The cheer left Kimberly. For a space of time, she'd been able to put Jack and their situation to the back of her mind. She shook her head. "He's much too busy. But thanks for taking Byron fishing. It's going to be the highlight of his vacation."

"Kim—"

"Devin, I don't want you to take time off to entertain me. I'm fully capable of being on my own."

"You spend too much time alone," he said. "But you have to understand that being the oldest, Jack always…" He sighed, searching for words. "We always took things in stride. And since we weren't the oldest, we weren't driven quite as hard. Jack was closer to Dad than the rest of us. He took on his drive and—"

"Whatever success he has will never be enough. He has to have more—to the exclusion of everything else," Kimberly finished for him. "I understand."

"But it doesn't make it easier for you. You know Janice and Mom will be there for you. We all will."

"Yes, I do, thank you very much. But I can deal with this baby alone."

"Kim—"

"Devin, I have to either accept things the way they are or make a change. *I* have to make a decision that doesn't include Jack. The most crucial thing I've learned through all this is I can't change him. I can only control what *I* do." She touched his hand. "I want to spend the next few days considering my options."

"You're pregnant, sis. You don't have any options."

"Oh, yes, I do."

Kimberly wanted to smile at the alarm crossing Devin's features. "Now, don't be hasty," he said. "You've been married seventeen years to my brother. That's a long time in this environment. You must have found something to love about him."

"I know how long I've been married."

They secured the boat and Devin drove Kimberly to the cabana.

"Kim, I will coach you through this delivery."

"Oh, Devin, you can't do that."

"It's not like Jack will do it. I don't want you to go through it alone. I'm going to take a vacation beginning a week before your due date."

Really touched, Kimberly touched Devin's cheek. "That's so sweet of you, but you're going to do that for your wife one day. I'll be fine. I'm an old hand at this now." Things got very personal in a delivery room, and Kimberly couldn't imagine baring all in front of Jack's brother.

"Thanks for the offer. It means so much to me." Kimberly slipped out of the car and knew Devin watched her until she closed the cabana door behind her.

Devin knew he had to intervene or his brother would find himself losing the best thing in his life. Jack was just too thickheaded to see farther than his nose.

You're going to do that for your wife one day. Kimberly had no idea how those words hurt. Byron and April were the closest to "his own" that Devin was ever likely to have.

Devin sighed. What to do? He beat out the tune of the music against the steering wheel. Kimberly's phone was on the seat beside him. He started to open the door, but checked the impulse. If Jack tried to call her cell phone he wouldn't reach her. And if he called the hotel's operator, Devin would have the operator dial a number that wouldn't be answered.

Devin chuckled at his own wit. It was time to show the old goat he had a few things to learn.

Jack should be on top of the world. Most of the things he wanted in life were in place. He'd won the blue ribbon for the new beer that would earmark the grand opening of the new brewpub.

He was being congratulated. Acquaintances and business associates took him out to dinner and drinks afterward. But he left early, not really in the mood for celebrating.

Now he lay in bed thinking of the many things to be done at home, but his mind kept veering to Kimberly and the kids. April hadn't called him once this week. It should be a good sign that she was enjoying the Caribbean. But she usually called him all the time, wanting to talk—even when she was in the Caribbean. Of course that could be a sign that she was growing up, but still... She was Daddy's little girl. They enjoyed a close relationship that he reveled in.

Of course, Kimberly gave him enough grief for several people, but she hadn't called him either, to complain or otherwise. But worse, she hadn't called him to let him know where she was.

Even now, he pictured her dancing on the beach, her face animated with laughter. Her perfume washing over him in the island breeze as he held her close, dancing. Jack closed his eyes. He imagined her soft body in his arms while they danced by the ocean, and his own body tightened with intense need.

He picked up the phone and dialed her cell number.

He just wanted to hear her sweet voice, but her cell phone immediately put him into voice mail. Kimberly's phone was never turned off, just in case one of the children needed her. Then he called the hotel's number. When the operator connected him, the phone rang and rang. When the message center came on he hung up before listening to the prerecorded drivel.

Kimberly hadn't even told him she was going to the island. That still hadn't sunk in. It was eleven-thirty, for God's sake! What was she doing that time of night? She usually went to bed early. She needed more sleep, now that she was pregnant.

A knot lodged in Jack's throat. He didn't expect to feel this need, this isolation, this sense of urgency. Why now, when he hadn't felt it before?

Jack frowned, lying back in the bed with his hands under his head. *He* should be fishing with his son and indulging April. *He* should be sailing with his wife.

In May, Devin had taken Kimberly snorkeling while Jack had worked on his proposal. And while she was on the beach alone, some guy was actually trying to pick her up. He'd always trusted Kimberly. That wasn't an issue. But was someone trying to pick her up now?

She wasn't showing. She was still a beauty.

An hour passed and Jack still hadn't fallen asleep. He punched the pillow and tried to call Kimberly again—and still received no answer. It was after midnight. Where the heck could she be?

"I'm sorry, Mr. Canter, I don't know where your wife is," the hotel's manager said.

What had he expected? To be met by everyone with open arms? So much for the first spontaneous, impulsive move of his adult life.

"What about Devin?"

The guy looked embarrassed. "He won't be back until tomorrow, sir."

"Tomorrow?"

"I'm afraid so. May I get you a room?"

"A key to my wife's room, please," he said.

As Jack was driven to the cabana, he thought of all the rescheduling he'd done to be with his family. And now everyone was away—even the kids.

He'd put Lauren in charge of keeping the wheels turning with the new pub. She would be presiding over meetings with the managers, meetings he should attend.

And Kimberly wasn't even at the hotel. She wasn't with the children. And Devin, his own brother, was suspiciously missing, too.

Jack's phone rang the next morning while he was pacing the floor, waiting for Kimberly and Devin to return. He snatched it up.

"Jack, get to the marina," Devin said. "A boat is waiting to take you to the main island. Kimberly's in the hospital. She was mugged and the guy hit her."

"Hell! How is she doing?"

"Just get to the hospital. I'm on my way there."

"You weren't with her?"

"No. I just got the call."

A thousand regrets flew through Jack's mind as he made his way to the hospital. A thousand what-ifs.

My God. His life would be nothing without her. Just knowing she was home—a place for him to come to—was enough.

He'd been a fool.

The hour it took to get to Kimberly was the longest hour of Jack's life.

He rushed into the hospital. Kimberly had a bandage on her head but she looked fine. Devin sat on the chair beside the bed, looking the worse for wear. His mother and his children were there as well.

"How is she?" Jack asked.

"She's going to be okay, but she's sleeping now," he whispered.

"And the baby?"

"Okay, too," Devin said, leading him out to the hallway. "She has to stay off her feet for a couple of days. I never should have let her go shopping alone. I should have been with her."

Jack dug his hands into his pockets. "That was my job."

"Yeah, it is, but where were you?" Devin said angrily.

"Everywhere I shouldn't have been."

"I'm glad you finally realized that. Or is this a crisis decision? What happens when everything is running fine again?"

"I know I've been focusing on the wrong things, okay?"

"That's nothing new." Devin swiped a hand across his face. "The whole family's made plans to be there when she has the baby. You don't have to bother. The family will take care of your wife if you won't."

"I'll be there for my wife," Jack said, angry that his family thought he wasn't responsible enough to look to the welfare and needs of his own wife.

"It shouldn't have taken an accident to make you see the light. I shouldn't have had to play games with you."

"Games?"

"Yes, games. I took Kim's cell phone so you couldn't reach her. I had the switchboard reroute her calls."

"You're interfering in something that's none of your business. You had no right to interfere with my calls to my own wife."

"What else would make you panic enough to come after her? You're here, aren't you? That says it all."

Jack bunched up his fists. "I should knock you flat on your ass."

Devin pounced on him. "You can try."

"Boys!" their mother said, coming between them, giving both of them stern looks. "This is a hospital, for heaven's sake. What's wrong with you?"

Jack regarded his brother and went back into the hospital room where Kimberly was still sleeping. He pulled up a chair beside the bed, gathered her hand in his, and sat.

When Kimberly awakened two hours later, Jack had nodded off.

"Jack?"

Jack awakened with a start. "How are you, baby?"

"I'm fine, except for a few aches. The baby's fine," she said. "The doctor's just taking precautions. Devin made sure of that."

Jack felt a stab of regret and something else—that his brother had to see to the welfare of his wife.

"How did you get here so quickly?" Kimberly asked.

"I was already here. I stayed in our cabana last night."

"What are you doing here?" Kimberly asked, puzzled.

He could do no more than tell her the truth. "I missed you."

"Missed me?"

"I've been without you too damn long, baby. I can't take this separation any longer."

"You've got a ton of work to do."

"Lauren's taking care of it. I decided it can get done without me."

"I think you need to be in this bed."

"I should have had my head examined a long time ago."

"You're feeling this way because you're afraid for the baby. But it's going to be fine."

"It's you I miss. As much as you don't believe that I love you and I would have married you anyway, it's the honest truth. After all is said and done, in the end it's going to be just us, babe. Just you and me."

"I want to believe you, Jack."

"I'm going to prove it to you."

Silence rang in the room for long moments.

"I was just so frightened I'd lose you," Kimberly said. "We were growing further and further apart. We even lived separate lives. I didn't know what to do to bring us back together. I never wanted a separation," she said. "But I realized at the island that if I wanted you I'd have to be willing to put up with your absences."

Jack squeezed her hand. "There won't be any more absences. I've been thinking a lot, and I know I have to make changes for you, because I'm not the best person I could be, and I want to be the best for you."

Kimberly regarded him as if she couldn't believe what she was hearing. "Do you really mean that?"

Jack nodded, knowing that he meant every word. It wouldn't be easy, but he was determined.

"Hey, slide over so I can hold you in my arms. Baby, I have to hold you."

Jack lifted Kimberly's back up and wrapped his hand lovingly around hers. She'd already snapped his head off several times after he'd said something inappropriate during contractions.

"Okay, push," Vicky said.

Kimberly pushed. And— *Christ Almighty!* She crushed his hand. It had to be broken. At the end of the contraction, Jack slid his hand away and shook it. She was paying him back for missing April's birth. But in reality, she didn't even know his hand hurt like hell.

"Here he comes," Vicky said, and out slid a red-faced, mucus-covered, wriggling thing of beauty.

Devin Canter II was born on February 28 at 11:58 p.m.

"Oh, God! Oh, God!" Words couldn't begin to express Jack's joy. "Look at what you've done, baby,"

Jack said to Kimberly. Her hair was a mess, but she was still the most gorgeous sight he'd ever seen. He had to hold her or burst. He gathered her tenderly in his arms and kissed her. The delivery had been long and hard and she was totally wiped out.

"Thanks for being here, Jack."

"Never thank me, baby. Thank you."

How could he not treasure this woman? Experiencing the birth of his child was better than any brewpub opening.

Epilogue

Their Mother's Day celebration was held in a meeting room at the brewpub this year, and both Jack's mother and Kimberly's were present as well as most of the rest of his family—and her mother's friend, Frank. Kimberly was overjoyed having all her family there. Even Lauren was present.

Kimberly never envisioned a friendship with the younger woman, but she'd grown to like her very much. As a matter of fact, one of Jack's brothers was eyeing her closely. Jack told her that he'd come into the brewpub often, mostly to catch sight of Lauren.

Jack had surprised her. He worked fewer hours now. And he took most weekends off. She actually had dinner with him most nights and most of the time they actually went to bed together. Kimberly never believed he could give up that much control of the pubs. But Jack being Jack, he still worried Lauren half to death. She seemed to take it in stride.

He eyed her now from the head of the table. She sat at the foot with Frank at her left. She'd enjoyed talking with him through the meal.

Jack had made a speech earlier a celebration of mothers and everyone had toasted. He'd ended with, "To mothers for their enduring love and devotion."

Jack's gaze met Kimberly's with love and desire, and her eyes misted.

Soon everyone left the table to mingle.

"Kimberly, why didn't you bring little Devin?" Jack's sister asked. "I would have held him."

"He was sleeping so I left him with the housekeeper." Jack had convinced her to hire a live-in. Kimberly found it convenient for times like these. It didn't intrude on her family life as much as she'd thought it would.

After Kimberly spoke to the rest of the family, he hustled them into the car and they headed home. Frank and her mother were spending the rest of the day with Jack's mother.

Little Devin was up and Kimberly played with him for a while before the housekeeper came for him. Needless to say, the older Devin was flattered beyond belief when he heard the baby was named after him.

"Is the little bugger asleep?" Jack asked.

"Of course not," Kimberly said. They both looked at little Devin as the housekeeper walked away. He had begun to fill out.

"He's going to break some woman's heart."

Kimberly eased Jack out the door and they went to their bedroom.

"Kim, I was never made more aware of how precious mothers are until after little Devin's birth. You give so much of yourself for the children, for me unselfishly. And we want you to know how much we appreciate you."

"Oh, Jack. Thank you. That's the best gift you could have given me."

"Okay." He took her shoulders between his hands. "Close your eyes." He turned her around. "Now you may open them."

Tears came to Kimberly's eyes. The children were holding a small sculpture of the family.

April was smiling and Byron held his father's satisfied look.

"Oh, you all."

Kimberly was so lucky. What a difference a year made. She never dreamed she could be so happy, that Jack would relax enough to spend more time with her and the children.

Later on, the kids went out and Jack put a soulful CD on the player. Sweet slow music piped into the room. "Do you remember what Vicky said?"

Kimberly frowned. "Did she say I needed to take more vitamins?"

Jack's crestfallen expression made her laugh. Kimberly walked into his arms and their bodies began to sway to the sweet music. Desire pooled in her middle. After complications, now that she'd had her final checkup, Vicky had given them the okay to make love again. "How could I not remember?" she said, reaching up to kiss him.

He swept her off the floor and headed to the bed.

Kimberly laughed. "This is my day. You don't get gifts."

"Just a tiny one?" Jack coaxed.

"Tiny! I expect great things from you, mister."

"Baby, your wish is my command."

Jack quickly stripped her of her clothes. "Baby, I'll take longer the second time. It's been a while."

Kimberly slid Jack's shirt from his shoulders and down his arms. "I don't intend to be shortchanged," she murmured in a stern voice.

Jack's self-satisfied smile made her laugh. "No doubt about it. My magic doesn't happen until my lady sings."

Kimberly closed her arms around his neck, bringing his lips to hers. The kiss was both erotic and sweet. "I'm so lucky," she whispered.

The desire in Jack's eyes left no doubt of where his thoughts veered.

Kimberly tapped him on the chest. "I'm not talking about sex."

Jack tilted her chin, the smile disappearing into a serious expression. "Neither am I, Kimberly. My life is richer, fuller and I have your stubbornness to thank for that."

"Stubbornness…"

"Enough talk, woman." Jack began to speak the language of desire and Kimberly relaxed to enjoy the pleasures of his touch.

REQUEST YOUR FREE BOOKS!
2 FREE NOVELS
PLUS 2 *FREE GIFTS!*

KIMANI ROMANCE™

Love's ultimate destination!

KROM08

The thirteenth novel in
the successful *Hideaway* series...

NATIONAL BESTSELLING AUTHOR

ROCHELLE ALERS

Secret Agenda

When Vivienne Neal's "perfect life" is turned
upside down, she moves to Florida to take a job
with Diego Cole-Thomas, a powerful CEO with
an intimidating reputation. Vivienne's job skills
prove invaluable to Diego, and on a business trip,
their relationship takes a sensual turn. But when
threatening letters arrive at Diego's office, he
realizes a horrible secret can threaten both of
them—and their future together.

"There's no doubt that Rochelle Alers is a compelling
storyteller who has the ability to weave romance with
the delicate subtlety of Monet."
—*Romantic Times BOOKreviews* on *HIDEAWAY*

*Coming the first week of May 2009
wherever books are sold.*

ARABESQUE®

www.kimanipress.com
www.myspace.com/kimanipress
KPRA I 350509